The Rules of Engagement

The Rules of Engagement

Published by The Conrad Press in the United Kingdom 2020

Tel: +44(0)1227 472 874
www.theconradpress.com
info@theconradpress.com

ISBN 978-1-913567-13-2

Typesetting and Cover Design by: Charlotte Mouncey, www.bookstyle.co.uk
Cover image created with authors own images

The Conrad Press logo was designed by Maria Priestley.

Printed and bound in Great Britain by Clays Ltd, Elcograf S.p.A.

The Rules
of Engagement

Chris Davies

for Cheltenham Saracens

Dear Shona

I'm writing you this letter at the start of the new season. Not an email, not a text message or a WhatsApp or anything else, but a proper old-fashioned letter. I think because at kick off I was somehow thinking of you and last summer, and that's far too much for anything other than a letter. And all these damn feelings are too much for a message.

Last year, after matches, I'd hurry home still pumped with adrenaline and chatty with drink, and you always wanted to hear about the game and who we'd played and all the stupid things the lads had got up to. Tonight I came home to an empty flat, and I thought – I don't know – maybe you'd still want to hear about the game. Maybe you'll read this and throw your head back in laughter. And even if you don't read it – even if I never send it – then maybe writing it down will make me feel less alone for a few minutes.

I was even thinking about you during the game. The smells of early summer – Deep Heat and fresh cut grass – now make me think of you. Fat blokes rubbing Deep Heat on their thighs and I'm thinking of you, bloody hell. We were playing Leyland and dominating them and my mind was wandering. I was thinking about the time you came to watch us, and you were wearing that halter-neck dress and your boots – were we playing Leyland that day too? And I snapped out of it because skip was yelling, 'Run the damn thing straight!' Our rotund prop took the pass at first receiver and did just that, carrying the ball straight into two defenders. You remember Mac? Kept his Movember tach past Christmas? They hit him simultaneously around his chest, wrapping up the ball and stopping any offload. Not that the fat bastard passes anyway. The slap of the tackle echoed across the field. He drove his legs for a few extra metres before a third defender tackled him around his knees, sending Mac crashing to the floor.

'That's one,' the referee called out, dropping back ten metres, 'held! Surrender! OK lads, stay on me, markers square!'

'X ball, second one up, then we play!' Yozzer called out. Our hooker, Jimmy, aligned himself behind the tackle, scanning the field. I knew what he was thinking, if the markers weren't square, he was going to hit that block hole behind the ruck and be gone. He's sneaky like that, loves a scoot.

The defender who took Mac's legs joined his defensive line, whilst the first two tacklers stood in at markers. Mac got to his feet and played the ball under his foot to Jimmy. We've got a new lad, in at second row and wearing eleven on his back, and he'd positioned himself at first receiver this time. Jimmy popped a pass to him and he ran straight, attempting a step at the last minute, trying to get an arm tackle and maybe half a break. But he wasn't agile enough: he's tall and bulky and the defenders read it. They wrapped him up and took him down to the ground. Decent run though.

'All right Jim, hit me, Y ball, Zack dummy drop off,' Yozzer said. I know you'll remember Yozzer cause when he streaked at the Christmas do the other year. Zack nodded at him in understanding. I watched from full back, standing five yards behind Yozzer. Jimmy fired the pass to him. He took it as Zack ran a line behind him and he faked the pass. The second receiver was another prop, Adders, another big lad. He came charging in on a hard line as Yozzer straightened his hips. He lifted a tiny pass to him which he took in his massive hands and ran towards the defence. He'd already picked out a target.

It was their half back, short, wiry and ginger, Yozzer's opposite number, who'd found himself out of position. Somehow, he'd ended up too far infield and Adders lined him up. The poor bastard couldn't even get his arms around him and he was sent flying backwards. Adders didn't even break stride as he gained an extra few metres before their big boys were able to tackle him. Supporters on the side lines cheered him on. We were now inside their half, further than I expected by third tackle.

'All right, let's play it now Jimmy!' Yozzer yelled out. I shifted across to the right and positioned myself behind our second half back. Jimmy fired the pass from dummy half to Yozzer, who had two big forwards running straight lines. Instead he passed the ball out the back of them. I set off in an arch behind two more forwards, Mac and Skip, and our half back once again played the pass out the back to me. I'd seen a gap, between their second row and centre. I was through it before the defence was able to close the hole. One of their quicker players, a bald fella playing at loose forward bore down on me and I got the pass away to our centre. He tried to step their full back, but the guy was good and tackled him before he could find our winger with an offload. The winger, Carl, small and pacey, went at dummy half. Carl found me with the pass, and I looked up. On the opposite side of the field there was space. Swifty, who's still playing on the wing and still me best mate, was waving his hands in their air. When he'd seen that I'd spotted him he pointed in front at the open space. I dropped the ball onto my foot, and it flew across the field. I watched as Swifty set his sights on it.

He only went and caught it on the full. I wish you'd seen it, Shona.

He did so at the ten-metre line. There weren't any defenders near him and Swifty had a free run in. The supporters on the other side of the barriers on Swifty's wing cheered. The clubhouse in that corner had further supporters on the balcony who joined in. I punched the air and clapped as Yozzer grabbed me around the neck.

'Cracking kick, Taz lad,' he said, ruffling my sweat-drenched hair.

A sea of orange surrounded Swifty to congratulate him, the yellow V's across their chests muddied, just like the player's arms and legs and faces. I turned around and saw Mac slowly making his way over, breathing hard, his hands on his hips.

'Taz pal, ask the ref how long's left, I'm dying here,' he panted. The ref was making his way from the in-goal area after awarding the try with Yozzer, as they prepared for the conversion.

'How long, sir?' I asked.

'That's the game,' the ref said.

'That's it, ya fat bastard,' I yelled back at Mac.

'Thank fook for that,' Mac said, turning to the sidelines, 'I'm gaggin' fer a pint.'

I walked to the rest of the team as Yozzer lined up his kick three yards in from the touchline. He hooked it, and it curled past the left post. It didn't matter, we'd already won, though Yozzer looked a little disappointed in himself. I think that was the only one he missed today. Mac waddled over to us and we formed two lines leading towards the changing rooms underneath the balcony, where our supporters were still clapping. The scoreboard up there read "Phoenix 28, Away 10". We started to clap as Leyland made their way through our players tunnel.

'Three cheers for Leyland Warriors,' Skip shouted 'Hip-hip.' You never really understood the whole tunnel thing, did you?

'H'RAY,' we chorused. We did this twice more and then Leyland formed their own tunnel and returned the gesture, clapping us into the changing rooms. I shook hands with my opposite number as I went past him. It all felt important at the time, but probably you don't care about any of this now.

In the changing room Mac had already pulled out a can of Stella from his kit bag. He'd removed his shirt and placed it neatly in the middle of the changing room, the number 8 barely visible beneath a layer of dried mud. Mac's stomach hung over the top of his shorts like a cupcake, red and swollen from the game.

'Cracking game lads,' he said as the rest of us joined him.

'Yeah, well done, boys,' Skip said. 'Anyone needing to see the physio see Andy now. We tried to get some bird from the college but instead we're stuck with this arsehole for another year!'

Andy was a small black lad doing a sports science course at St Helens College. He was with us last year (though I doubt you ever met him) and we took the piss, but the lad's a miracle worker. He's about five-five but gives a massage that could roll out dried concrete. I mean, not a massage like you used to do, obviously, but the next best thing. I went over to Swifty before I started to get changed.

'Solid finish, pal,' I said, as we slapped hands and embraced, patting each other's backs.

'Mate, I didn't know if you'd seen me,' he replied, 'pin-point kick, I tell thee, better than Yozzer.'

'He wishes,' Yozzer said, dumping his shirt in the pile with little care.

'Bloody hell, Yoz, get it the right way round at least; my missus goes mental when they aint right!' Skip said, picking up the shirt and pulling the arms through so it was the right way around. Yozzer's number 6 shirt was pretty much in the same clean state as when he put it on.

'Don't worry, Skip. Don't need to wash Yozzer's, lewk at it, he didn't make a tackle all game!' Carl joked and he placed his shirt in the pile and like Mac's, his number 2 was under a layer of mud.

'Piss off Carl, I ran that game!'

'You're a soft shite!'

'And how many did you get today, pal?

'You only scored because Lard-arse over there can't run more than ten metres and had to give to you!' Carl gestured at Mac, who had cracked open a second can of Stella and removed his shorts, so he sat bollock naked next to the new second rower, who looked increasingly uncomfortable.

'How'd you find that, Newbie?' Skip yelled across the changing room.

'Enjoyed it, mate. Tough though,' he said.

'Warriors are hard, to be fair. It's Harry, yeah?'

'Yeah, Harry. Do you want the shorts back?'

'Nah mate. Gizza tenner and you keep shorts n socks. Wash fer next week though, Newbie!'

Newbie smiled. He seemed content with the nickname. I stripped off my shorts and shoved them, along with my Nike boots and team socks, into a drawstring bag and then tossed the bag into my larger Sutton Phoenix holdall. I took some L'Oréal "5-in-1" shower gel and my towel and headed to the showers. The shower room had twelve showers around the outside walls and a few players were in there already, including our new six-foot-two, two-hundred-pound Samoan centre Manny, who we've cleverly nicknamed "Samoa".

'Here he is, with his "5-in-1"!'

'You got the "5-in1"? Give us some, pal?' Jimmy asked across the shower room. He stepped towards me and I squeezed some of the gel directly onto his head. Jimmy stepped back under the water and began to wash his hair. I turned on the shower next to Samoa and started to wash myself. Two Leyland Warriors were on the other side of the room cleaning mud off their knees and elbows. Samoa removed the strapping he had on his right knee and scrunched it up into a ball. He then turned to face Jimmy, whose head was back as he continued to wash his hair. Samoa lobbed the ball of tape straight at his balls, catching him square in his nutsack.

'Fuck me!' Jimmy grabbed himself, doubling over. Samoa and I burst out laughing and high-fived each other. Even the Leyland players laughed as Jimmy breathed deeply, spitting towards the drain in the middle of the room. Skip entered and turned on the shower next to mine.

'Stop pissin' about lads. Get showered and get upstairs,' he said.

'Sorry Skip,' I said, still laughing. Samoa patted Jimmy's shoulder.

'That were fer the hospital pass in first half, dickhead!'

I washed my hair and my arms, legs and face, then returned

to the changing room. The Taz of Tasmania tattoo on my right arm had a scratch just beside it. You know, I still don't regret getting it done. It's why they call me Taz, and I kind of like that nickname. I put on a pair of chinos and slipped on some brown deck shoes, then my after-match shirt. It was white, with an orange Phoenix logo over the left breast. I took some hair clay and went to the mirror above the sink in the toilets to sort myself out. From the toilet cubicle I heard a flush and Yozzer came out.

'Come on, ya poofty, I'm gagging fer a pint,' he said.

'I'll see you up there, pal,' I was concentrating on getting my hair just right. When I was content, I washed my hands, grabbed my gear and walked around the side of the club house. At the bottom of the stairs was a pile of bags left by players, which I tossed mine onto, then I ascended the stairs and entered the clubhouse bar. It's the same as it always was: a pool table at one end and the bar at the other, running perpendicular to the terrace doors that lead to the balcony. Down the other side, opposite the bar, the row of tables with lounge chairs, decorated with old Sutton shirts – the ones they sometimes move to make room for a skittle ally. Next to the bar, in "Port Corner" the table with a bell above. I went over to the bar to join Yozzer and Swifty.

'Here y'are.' Swifty passed me a pint of Boddy's.

'Cheers pal. You getting on it tonight?'

'Maybe. There's the social next week so thinking just a few here tonight, then go hard next weekend, go into town like.'

'Sound mate,' I took three large gulps of the Boddingtons. We stood by the bar and drank, not saying much, just hydrating with beer. Then Skip went over to the bell and rang it.

'Leyland, your tea's up,' he shouted across the bar. The Leyland players made their way to the food hatch opposite the stairs.

'Who did the food today?' Yozzer asked.

'How should I know?' I replied.

'It was Mac's missus I think; she done a chilli,' Swifty said.

'She does a mint chilli,' I said. After a few minutes, Skip rang the bell again.

'All right Phoenix, your tea's ready.'

Yozzer, Swifty and I joined the queue at the food hatch and got our food. Swifty was right. It was chilli and rice. We took the polystyrene trays of food back into the clubhouse and sat at a table to eat.

'Anybody going to the Saints game on Thursday?' Yozzer asked.

'I could be keen. Who's it against?' I asked.

'Warrington. It's on telly like, but I could get us tickets and have a couple of bevvies afterwards.'

'I got work early on Friday. I can't get blindo,' Swifty said, shovelling rice into his mouth.

Well, to be honest, I don't go out as much these days. It's not the same when I don't have you to meet afterwards. So I made my excuses: 'Me too and there's the social next Saturday. I wanna save money for that.'

'Oh I didn't mean get hammered, just go Punch Tarmey or something after.'

'Yeah All right, sounds good.'

From Port Corner the bell rang again. Skip was back with the Leyland captain. An array of drinks had been laid out on the table under the bell.

'Right lads, listen up Man of the Match time,' Skip bellowed. 'First up I think he had a cracking game, Leyland's half back, number seven.'

'Danny, that's you pal,' the Leyland captain pointed at the Warriors' half back. Their team cheered as Danny marched up to Port Corner. 'And for you lads, some barnstorming runs and crunching tackles, Phoenix number eight.'

I put two fingers in my mouth and whistled as the rest of the team clapped. Mac joined the Leyland halfback in Port Corner.

'Okay, a couple more. We had a debutant, Harry, come on up here lad.' Skip beckoned Newbie to join him and we cheered and clapped 'and one more, Dickhead of the Day, for thinking we were on the fifth when we weren't and panicking, trying to kick even though he's a fat bastard and can't kick... Mac!'

The club house erupted. I whistled again, along with Swifty this time; the rest of the team got to its feet to applaud Mac. He put his hands on his rotund hips and shook his head at Skip, who just laughed.

'All right lads, it's a port each for the man of the match, followed by a pint of lager. Newbie, a port for you for a debut and Mac, you get the Shit Mix!'

The Leyland half back picked his port and lager, Newbie was handed his shot of port, and Mac given a shot of port, a pint of lager, and a pint glass filled with various other alcoholic drinks. Skip rang the bell again.

'Get it down ya, lads!'

All four downed their ports, then Mac and the Leyland halfback chugged down their pint of lager, turning it upside down above their heads when they finished. Mac belched and prepared himself as the club house cheered him on. A black plastic bin had been placed front of him. He raised the glass in a toast to the watching crowd.

'UP THE PHOENIX!' he yelled and opened his mouth wide, gulping the mixture down his throat. The crowd continued to whoop and holler and cheer. He reversed the empty glass above his head again and the cheers got louder.

Then he threw up in the bin.

It was a disgusting colour of purple from the port and gold from the lager. It would have made you want to vom too, Shona. I can still smell the aniseed of the sambuca. Yozzer and Swifty were laughing their arses off.

'Well done lads, enjoy the night!' Skip called out. A few players clapped as we all went back to our own drinks and conversations.

'Anyone up for a game of nails?' Samoa approached us and placed his hand on my shoulder.

'Oh aye, yeah, I'll play.'

'Go on then, I'll 'ave a game,' Yozzer said, finishing his pint, 'Swifty get us a nail when you get the round in.

'Int it Taz's round?'

'Fuck off Swifty, ya cheap arse, just get us a beer!'

'Fine! How many nails?'

'It's us four, Newbie, Coach and Big Kev, so seven' Samoa said, 'get the hammer as well.'

Nails is a pretty simple game. Did I ever tell you about that one? Out on the balcony we've got a log that's about the size of a large beside table in circumference and about three foot in height. Comes up to around my belly button, anyway. What we do is take a nail and hammer it in gently so it stands about four inches or so out of the log. Then, using a chisel-head hammer, not the flat part (unless you're a girl, so if you had come up we would have let you), you get one stroke to try and hit the head of your nail. The last person to hammer their nail completely into the log has to buy a round of port for the rest of the players. Simples.

You'll remember that port is the club drink, sort of a tradition we have at Sutton.

We stood in a circle around the log and prepared our nails. Swifty got to go first, because he got the nails and hammer. He missed by a good few inches, but it was a hard shot and the thin edge of the chisel got stuck in the wood. Swifty tugged it out. Like any other turn taking game, the hammer moved to the left. This meant it was my turn. I missed as well, though not as spectacularly as Swifty. I passed the hammer to Yozzer. He's good at this game and sure enough he connected with the nail, plunging it an inch into the log.

'Yes, Yozzer,' I said, patting his shoulder. The game continued. Newbie was surprisingly good, seeing as he'd never played before, and he hit the nail but not very hard. Samoa missed and then so did Big Kev, our second rower. Coach airshot, meaning he missed the log entirely which called for a big cheer and laughter at his expense ('shut it or I'll get you doing laps!'). Swifty made an absolute meal of his next shot. He missed the nail and the log almost completely. He scratched the edge and a piece of bark fell off and onto the floor.

'Wayyyy! Log damage, drink up!' Samoa commanded. The rule is, if you chip any of the bark away like that you have to down your drink. It also means you have to buy yourself a new drink, regardless of the round you're in.

Like you always said: rugby players are idiots.

Yozzer was the first to get his nail in; he's so good he only missed once. Newbie shocked everyone and finished second and I came third. Samoa, Big Kev, Coach and Swifty battled it out, but there was only going to be one loser. Big Kev and Samoa went out in the same round, leaving Coach and Swifty.

It took so long for those two to go head-to-head that Yozzer and myself were able to have an extra beer before Coach finally sank his nail. Swifty, reluctantly, although inevitably, went to the bar to order a round of port for us. We cheered and downed them.

The juke box had started playing and a few players were filtering out. Leyland had left ages ago and it was pretty much the starting thirteen left. On the TV screens there was a Super League game on. It looked like Hull versus Wigan but seeing as we all hate Wigan no one was really paying attention, except for a couple of old boys who watched the game and were sticking around. Swifty, Yozzer and I waited for one rendition of Neil Diamond's version of *Sweet Caroline,* our unofficial club song, which we sang with much gusto. Then we called a taxi, said our farewells and headed home. It was only eight, but I planned on ordering a Chinese and relaxing.

The taxi dropped Swifty off first at his place near St Helens' stadium, then Yozzer a little further on. I'm in the middle of town, these days, in a piece of shit one-bedroom apartment above the Golden Dragon Chinky. I payed what was left of the fare (about a fiver) and headed through the door and up the stairs next to the takeaway. I entered my apartment and chucked my kit onto the floor next to my sofa. I ordered through Just Eat and then I slobbed down on the sofa and stared at the blank television screen across the sparse living room. The table in the centre still housed a few empty beer cans.

Alone again. I don't know why I've written all this. I just meant to write a quick note but I've been at it for hours. I know you won't care. But at least it's late now, and I feel like I might finally be ready to sleep.

I wonder what you're up to? If I do send this, would you write me back your news?

Jamie

***

Sunday, May 7th

Weight:	86.5Kgs
Instagram Posts:	Zero
Medication:	200mg Sertraline
Food:	Leftovers
Suicidal Thoughts:	One so far

Dear Shona,

When I woke up I read through all what I wrote last night. God knows what I was thinking. I guess it was just the booze and that, but writing to you was – what do they say? – cathartic or something, even if I feel like a right dickhead this morning.

But it's half nine and all I've been doing is staring at the ceiling. You must remember the ceiling colour, though to be fair your eyes were closed when you were on your back. There was absolutely nothing interesting about it; no stains, no Blue Tac marks, no cracks in the paintwork from previous tenants, no posters that I'd put up, not even a spider traversed its way on a dangerous, inverted mission.

Nothing. Nada. Niente.

And yet I continued to stare.

I checked my phone again, but no new messages. Not even a Facebook notification or a spam email. I contemplated texting one of the lads, even to the point of opening a new message, but I locked the screen and tossed the phone to the end of my double bed. Yozzer spent Sundays at his Nan's having a family roast (I'd been invited a couple of times, but felt awkward so declined) and Swifty, well to be honest I never knew what

Swifty got up to on a Sunday. Every now and then I think he went to a driving range, at least that's what his Instagram story said. I rolled over and bit a hangnail on my middle finger. You used to hate me doing that.

I've been awake for the past hour but had zero motivation to move. I've been through Facebook three times and Instagram twice, to the extent I've seen the "You're all caught up" message. You haven't posted anything in days. Or have you blocked me?

Sundays are my rest day, so I don't go to the gym. This is mainly because my body needs a day off, but also because after a game I feel like I've been body slammed by a sumo wrestler.

Listen, Shona. I've been on two-hundred milligrams of sertraline, the antidepressant, for the past three months, but I have to admit I don't like them. Before that I tried citalopram and Prozac. Now I'm thinking about going back to citalopram. Maybe I'll talk to the doctor about it. In my drawer are a couple of months' worth of pills though, so I'll probably just do it myself, ween off the sertraline and back onto the citalopram.

Do you know about any of these things?

Yozzer is the only person who knows I take them and he only found out by accident. We were having a night out about a week ago and I'd managed to get hold of some cocaine from one of the other players. I'd stored it in my drawer and Yozzer went to get the drugs and found all my pills. I told him that I was just getting anxious because work was stressful, and rugby was tough.

I didn't tell him that I'd been on the pills for over a year because without them I used to think about all the ways I could kill myself.

I always thought I'd be elaborate about it. Get one of my

grandpa's shotguns from the farm, walk into the middle of St Helens, stick it into my mouth and blast my brains out the back of my head.

I researched how to tie a tourniquet properly so that I could hang myself from the light fixing in my bedroom. But I found two problems with that. Firstly, my apartment was a piece of shit and the light would most certainly be unable to take my weight. Secondly, I had a shite gag reflex. I'd throw up, choke on my own vomit and be found looking like the biggest dick-head in Merseyside.

Other options I thought about were slitting my wrists, but I got a papercut once and ever since then had been squeamish of sharp objects. Then there was getting a hose, attaching it to the exhaust pipe of my beat-up old Ford Capri and gassing myself. But knowing my luck the heap of shit would probably conk out on me. Serves me right eh, how many times did you tell me to sell that 'heap of junk' and get something new?

Once I bought a bottle of undiluted bleach and even got so far as to put it in a pint glass. The smell made me throw up and I cried like a fairy, my head balanced on the toilet seat.

Look, I'm not saying this is all because you left. But I'm not saying it didn't have an impact. Of course it did. You were… are the love of my life. Maybe one day you'll know how this feels. I mean I don't want you to feel bad. Or maybe I do. Maybe I want you to feel something, anything, a bit of guilt, so you can feel as bad as I do. But then I feel bad for getting so angry. Jesus Shona, my head is a mess, a real mess.

I didn't contemplate OD'ing until I started taking the head pills. Ironic as the suicidal thoughts went away after a while. It was after the bleach episode that I went to see the doctor and had a little chat. He said rugby was good for me, and since then I started going to the gym as well. I'm not as skinny as I was when you dated me but still small, and when I started I was offered steroids, and still was every now and then. I was uming and ahhing over whether I wanted to start or not. I wasn't arsed about the legality, I guess I was just nervous. But when I looked in the mirror, I didn't like what I saw. My pecks were flat, there was no definition in my abs and my arms could be so much bigger. I wondered if you would have liked me to be bigger. I always did wonder what it was that you first saw in me. You could have had anyone. Wasn't your ex a bodybuilder or something?

The doctor also gave me the number of a counselling service, but I never got around to calling them. I didn't like talking to my friends about my feelings, so why they would I talk to some guy I didn't know? I mean, did you have any idea all this was going on in my head? Maybe you did, somewhere deep down.

Anyway, listen, just now as I was writing this, my phone pinged: it was Derek, the guy from the gym; 'I have a new shipment in, £30 for a month, £75 for 3, you want?'.

So I got up and went to the bathroom. I had slept in a pair of Oddballs, those England ones you liked me in, and I flexed in front of the mirror. I'm just not big enough, no matter how hard I work out. I went back through to my bedroom. Sod it.

'Yeah man, give me 3 months' worth,' I typed back.

'Good lad. Go to the pharmacy and ask for a needle exchange. Make sure you get a new one each week. I'll show you the first time if you want.'

I typed back 'Ok,' and tossed the phone back onto my bed. I guess that's it for now, Shona. I probably won't send this.

Jamie

***

Sunday, May 7th (again)

Activities:	Laundry
Weight:	86.5Kgs
Instagram Posts:	Zero
Medication:	200mg Sertraline
Food:	Left overs
Suicidal Thoughts:	One

Dear Shona,

Sorry, I didn't mean to write again, but something weird just happened: I just found something of yours.

After I finished your last letter, I realised I had to tidy up. The floor was a mess. Clothes lay scattered around, the wardrobe door was ajar and my kit bag had been dumped by my bedroom door. The Under Armour compression shorts would be starting to smell and you know how bad they get.

But I had no motivation: I flopped back onto my bed and returned to my ceiling watching.

It was still cream.

One hour passed.

Then a second.

Before I knew it, it was midday. My stomach rumbled, so I rolled out of bed, picked up a pair of Adidas tracky bottoms and put them on. Ironically I think they were a pair you bought me. Then I went through to my living room/dining room/kitchen. The left-over char sui chow mien beckoned me, so I tipped it out of the foil container and onto a plate, whacked it in the microwave and heated it up. Yes, I know you said that heating up old Chinese is bad for me, but you can testify to how bad my cooking is. I turned on the telly and channel hopped until the microwave pinged. I removed the chow mien, sat on the still-stained two-seater sofa and watched *Catchphrase*. When I was done, I tossed the dish into the sink (sod it, I'd do it later) and returned to my bedroom.

Come on you lazy bastard, washing.

I grabbed my wicker washing basket, which was only half full, from the corner of my room. I proceeded to look around, sniffing various items of clothing to see if they needed to join the wash. A World Gym string vest, yep. The odd sock or two, most definitely. A pair of grey Calvin Klein's, they'd last another day.

I looked down the side of my bed and spotted another pair of boxer shorts. I reached for them and managed to get my fingertips onto the hem. Pulling them out, I gave them a sniff.

Wow, they'd been down there for a while. In the basket they went. Then, something caught my eye. It glinted in the midday sun that had crept in through a crack in the curtains. I reached out and clawed my fingers around whatever it was. Holding it up, I recognised it almost instantly. It was an earring.

Fuck.

It was yours.

Yeah, definitely, I was sure this is the one you said you'd lost, the one your mum got you for Christmas. I really wasn't in the mood for this. Was anyone ever in the mood for this? Thinking about you is one thing, but actually finding something of yours...

Ah, I really didn't need this today.

My arse found the bed once more and again I leaned forward.

This time, I played with your earring.

Another hour passed.

Finally, I placed it on my bedside table. Yeah, I know, it was bringing back all these feelings for you and making me feel like shit, but I was gonna keep it. Messed up, innit?

I had a washer-drier in my kitchen now, a second hander given to me from Yozzer's mum. Not the best in the world, but it sure beat the Hell out of trekking to the laundrette and spending two pound a wash and two pound a dry. Especially now that I didn't get to do that with you anymore. Grab an all-day brekkie from the café down the road. I lobbed a gel pod in and threw in a load of darks. I was about to press start when I remembered my rugby kit.

'Damnit,' I muttered, traipsing back to bedroom and grabbing my kitbag. Your earring eyed me up. Back in the kitchen, I set the washing on and slobbed on the sofa. *Catchphrase* had ended and now an old episode of *Starsky and Hutch* was playing. I still liked my old cop shows, so I left it on and let the thought of you intrude my mind.

You just up and left me. 'Didn't love me anymore'. What the hell does that mean, Shona? How do you just stop loving someone? You gave me some other excuses, I needed to sort myself out, the sex was going downhill. The thing that pissed me off the most though, all those things we could have sorted out if you'd actually spoken to me about them.

'It's too late now, Jamie,' you said, 'I just don't think I love you anymore.'

And that was that. I loved you. I still do. It hurts like hell, but that's life. I've not had the best of luck with women. I'm not a bad guy, like I don't cheat or nothing, guess I just make mistakes.

Except one, Shelley, who cheated on me.

Bitch.

But I thought you and I might make it. I was an old romantic, I think. Guess I was wrong. On the telly, Huggy Bear is making an appearance. I fucking hate Sundays.

Jamie.

***

Monday, May 8th

Work:	8:30 until 5
Gym:	5:30
Weight:	86.6Kgs
Current Bench Max:	120Kgs
Current Dead Lift Max:	200Kgs
Instagram Posts:	3 training, 1 selfie
Food:	chicken and broccoli x 3
Suicidal Thoughts:	Zero

Dear Shona,

I feel like I'm falling into a routine of these letters now. I kind of like it. It's like I'm still talking to you. God knows if I will send them, but up here, in my head, it feels like we are still talking. And I like that. Anyway, now a new week is starting.

I start back on the diet on Mondays, which I try to follow all week, and I have to go back to my dog shite job in a dog shite warehouse. It's a furniture shop, so all day all I do is check the stock, drive a forklift and help pack the lorries. All day. Every day.

Five days a week.

But it pays the bills. I'm smart, you know I didn't go to college or nothing. I don't think I ever told you about golf though. So remember when I said that I didn't get any good GCSE's? at the time it didn't bother me, because I was so good at golf. Don't get me wrong, I loved rugby back then as well, I was a half back first, then a full back. But golf, I don't know, it chilled me. I could have gone pro, no doubt. My arsehole dad never took me, so I would get the bus and play after school and on weekends. I saved up and bought a second-hand set of clubs. Ping ones, so decent, the three wood had a chip and the putter was a little bent. But they were good.

I won tournaments. Should have seen me, I was like Rory McIlroy. At school, no one gave a shit, I was ok but not amazing at rugby, my grades were all D's and E's, but on the course I was someone. But then the parents found out. You want to know why you never met them, Shona, well this is why. They told the school, the school said it was affecting my grades. They made me bring my clubs home (I had convinced the course to store them for me) and sold them. Or gave them to some charity shop. Probably sold, my parents didn't do nothing for nobody. So that were it. I got like five GCSE's and moved out the moment I was sixteen. Don't think I've ever told you any of that. Never liked to talk about it.

Straight after school I got a job packing shelves at the local Tesco, then I worked for a carpenter for a few years when I met you. Then onto this job; Warehouse Assistant. That was my full title. But it should have been "Warehouse Bitch" because I swear to God I did bloody everything in that place. I got my head down and got on with it, though. I didn't complain to colleagues, I just put on my green polo every morning and went in. Then, at five o'clock, I punch out and go to my second favourite place, after the rugby club.

Olympia isn't anything special, but it's better than the big gyms in town, like that DW you used to go to (still go to?). They're full of posers, lads that did a few reps then checked out their bodies in the mirrors. Oh, but they would only do that if there were some girls nearby, obviously, or what would be the point? I hated guys like that. Always thought you'd leave me for one like that. Tattooed and bronzed. I wanted to stick my headphones in and just get on with it, which is what I could do at Olympia. I like to post on social media though, so I suppose I'm a bit of a hypocrite. Though of my sixty-odd followers most were rugby lads, barely any women followers. Don't think you follow me anymore, do you?

Monday was chest day. It made up for the shitty day at work. Just a shame I always had to wait until around five-thirty to start the session. First, I did five sets of ten bench press at eighty kilograms. This warmed my chest up and gave a nice stretch at the bottom of the press. Then, three sets of ten dumbbell flies with fifteen kilograms each hand, which really opened my pectoral muscles up. Finally, seated chest push on the cables, increasing the weight each time, but reducing the reps on each set. It gave me a nice chest burn. I loved it. That was my favourite exercise. Arnie used to say that the pump he got from working out was better than coming. I don't know if I'd say it was that good, but it sure was awesome. As I write it now, I wonder if any of that has even sunk in with you. You know me, when I get into something I go into far too much detail. As I was finishing up, Derek approached me.

'Come into the changing rooms when you're done, lad,' he said. I finished my last set, swigged some water from a large tankard-style bottle, wiped the sweat from my forehead and headed for the changing rooms.

They were small, with three showers in individual cubicles at the far end. It had just one toilet cubicle, which trust me you did not want to use, especially after one of the big boys had been in. Caffeine, protein and steroids play havoc with their bowels. Twelve bright red lockers (the colour scheme of the gym) were against the left wall and a bench ran along the right and sat on it, was Derek.

He was a big old lad. Must have weighed around one-hundred-and-thirty kilograms, at least. He was wearing a baggy (must have been XXXXL) Everlast gym vest and matching black knee length shorts. Tattoos of tribal designs, dragons and warriors were painted over bulging muscles on his arms and legs, and his veins stood out from his skin like train tunnels. His head was shaved, his nose broken and eyes dark brown. On the bench was a large cardboard box of vials and pills. I went over to the locker I'd used to store my stuff and took off the padlock.

'You get a needle?' Derek asked.

'Got it on my lunch mate.'

'Good lad. Right, let's get you started on Test. You ain't never used any roids before right?'

'No.'

'Well then let's not fuck about too much to start mate.' Derek pulled out a small vial of clear liquid. On the side it read "Testosterone".

'Here,' I said, passing Derek a brand-new needle I'd gotten from the pharmacy. The lady behind the counter didn't say anything when I asked. She gave me this pack that had a plastic spoon in it as well. You would be horrified if you knew how easy doing crack is.

'Cheers. Right let's be quick, Joe doesn't give a shit but some of the older blokes in here might take offence.' Derek took off the protective end from the needle and inserted it into the vial. 'So, we'll start you on two-hundred milligrams. Once you've got it always tap the needle mate and push a little out, that way you won't get any air bubbles. Now, get yer arse out.'

I pulled down my shorts and boxers to just below my arse cheeks and leaned against the bench. I was a little nervous and I think Derek could tell. He tapped the needle and squirted a tiny bit of the liquid out.

'Clench a little mate,' he said, 'magic, right now relax. Good.'

I barely felt the needle go into my right cheek. It was like a tiny scratch. I had a strange light-headed sensation for a moment, and then it was over. I took the alcohol swab that Derek offered me and wiped away the tiny droplet of blood before I pulled up my pants.

'Here,' he handed me the used needle and the vial, 'get a fresh needle every time, that's how you get yourself in trouble, AIDs and all that shit. Take it to the pharmacy and replace it. Two-hundred milligrams, and that's a week, remember. After a while we'll up it to four-hundred, OK?'

'OK.'

'Don't fuck about with it, then we can look at other shit for ya, get you on Tren or something, get you absolutely massive.'

'Cheers mate,' I placed the protective end back on the needle and put them into my Phoenix rucksack. Just as I turned to leave, Derek stopped me.

'Hey up, lad, aren't you forgetting something?'

'Ahh, sorry mate, here,' I took out my wallet and handed over the cash to him. I've got the feeling he'd be able to crush me with one hand if I didn't pay him.

'I'll see you later mate. I'll be doing arms Wednesday if you wanna join?'

'Yeah mate, sounds good,' I left the gym with everything.

Does it make you think any less of me that I've tried steroids? I'd love you to see me looking my best. Maybe it would make you want me back. I suppose I can only hope. And as for the golf stuff, I bet you're wondering why I never played whilst we were together. Too many bad memories, I guess. I reckon I could still be good, but I hate the sport. Rugby has my heart now.

Jamie.

***

Wednesday, May 10th, St Helens

Workout done:	Arms with Derek
First:	3x10 Bicep Curls
Second:	3x10 Hammer Curls
Third:	5x20 Skull Crushers
Fourth:	3x10 Triceps Pushdowns
Fifth:	Isolated Curls
Finisher:	21 Inch Gun Salute

Dear Shona,

The problem with working out with Derek was that he is so huge but so dense he thinks that I'm able to lift the same amount he can. Don't get me wrong, the man knows what he is doing, whilst he is a roid-head he still has to work out to get to his size and definition. But the weights he got me lifting; damn. It was a nice pump, but I couldn't straighten my arms at all. Whenever I tried they were so swollen that they just retracted back to an angle. I'd agreed to go the pub with Swifty and Yozzer after the session as well. There was a large chance I'd get there and not be able to lift a pint. Saying that, I got the feeling you'd love to see my new muscular arms. Or at least, I like to think you would love them.

Of course, that was just me being silly. I went home, showered, then put on a Ralphie polo (Maybe those fashion tips you gave me had paid off a little) and went to meet the boys at The Wheatsheaf. Yes, I know, we drank at the bloody Wheatsheaf. But what can I say, you hated it, we liked it. I walked down and left my car on the back street near my flat. I didn't want to get pulled over after a couple of pints. Never worth the hassle. Like when we almost got done after Sally's leaving do. It was around eight o'clock, the sun was looking to set and there was that nice, warm spring air. When I got there, Yozzer was waiting at the bar, two pints of Guinness being placed in front of him as I walked in through the door.

'Where's Swifty?' I asked.

'Hey pal, he said he wasn't feeling it, having a long week at work I think so just going to chill at home cause we got Thatto on Saturday and the social and blah blah.'

'Fair enough, maybe he's got a bird with him. Cheers pal,' I said as Yozzer handed me a pint.

'Ha, yeah right, this is Swifty we're talking about!'

'Yeah, you're right, poor bastard.'

'That boy just needs to get laid.'

'As much as I hate to agree with you, I think you're right for once,' I said. If you'd seen what Swifty has been like this past couple of months I reckon even you would be saying the same.

The pint tasted good. Yozzer had got the extra cold and because I was still quite out of breath, I drank a fair bit with the first swig. Thing with Guinness is it's surprisingly thirst quenching, which isn't what most people find with it. Each to their own, I suppose. You absolutely hated it.

'How are you doing anyway, pal?' Yozzer asked me. We had moved from the bar to a table across the pub.

'Yeah mate, I'm OK.'

'Just OK?'

'I mean I'm good, yeah I'm good.'

'You aint telling me something.'

Bloody friends. They just know, didn't they? He was the only person I could talk to about you.

'I found an earring on Sunday in me room,' I said.

'You aint got pierced ears?'

'No shit! It were Shona's, weren't it.'

'Oh. Oh! Shona's.'

'Just got me thinking about her.'

'When were the last time you spoke to her?'

'Months mate, months. I mean, I'm over her like, I think I am.'

I was lying to him. Of course I was. Here I am writing a letter to you about how I was telling my best mate I was over you. The sound of Boston's *More Than a Feeling* played over the sound system, probably from some Classic Pub Playlist on Spotify.

Could we be more of a stereotype?

'Ah, fuck Shona, mate,' Yozzer eventually said. Sorry, he's blunt is Yozzer.

'I seem to recall that being your advice when I first met her.'

'And was I right?'

'No! I got a broken heart and multiple headaches!'

'Oh, stop being such a tart, it weren't that bad!'

'I suppose.'

Another moment of quietness between us. Boston had finished and now Thin Lizzy had started singing *Whiskey in the Jar*.

'Was she any good?' Yozzer asked me about you. I didn't know how much I wanted to tell him about our sex life.

'Any good at what?'

'Sex.'

'Bloody hell, mate!'

'I'm just curious, were she?'

'I mean, yeah she were decent..'

'Really?' he asked.

'She never wanted to get on top.'

'Like, never got on top?'

'Well, once or twice, but never for long, she just liked missionary mainly.'

'Well that's boring!'

'Yeah, yeah I suppose it was, to be fair!'

'See! You're better off without her!'

'Because the sex was boring?'

'Yes! Mate, I know it sounds superficial, or shallow, or whatever, but that's the way it is. Look at this way, you want a relationship, you want to meet someone, fall in love, get married etc. etc?'

'Yeah, I do.'

'Well then, you can't be with someone you have boring sex with! Like it or not sex is a massive part of it, and if there's no sexual chemistry, or its boring, then things will fizzle and you'll never make it work, cause things are shit in every department!'

'How is it, you're right, like every time, with relationships, yet you refuse to get involved?'

'The sooner you guys realise I'm a genius, the better,' Yozzer sat back in his chair and finished his pint.

'I think that's going a bit far, pal!' I looked down at my empty glass.

I'm sorry I spoke to Yozzer about our sex, but you have to admit, you *hated* going on top. I got the feeling you felt self-conscious, which was a real shame because I loved looking up and seeing your gorgeous body grinding on me. I could hold your curvy hips and ass (which, by the way, I loved and haven't seen better since) and move in motion with you. When you did get on top you were louder, I swear.

This is what frustrates me, Shona. This is something we could have worked on. We could have talked, I could have made you love your body and that sex that you said went downhill would have shot back up (no pun intended). But you just used it as an excuse. Was there someone else, is there someone else? Actually, I don't want to know. I'd rather just go to bed tonight with the image of you fucking me. I'll have sweet dreams now, for sure.

Jamie.

***

Thatto Heath Crusaders A v Sutton Phoenix, May 13ᵗʰ

Starting Position:	Full Back
Food:	Porridge
Instagram Posts:	One
Instagram Likes:	Twelve
Test Injected:	200mg
Suicidal Thoughts:	Two

Dear Shona,

Second game of the season and yet again I was thinking about you. Maybe this was why I was playing so shit. The weather was a bit muggy as well, but the Crusaders were playing in the same conditions so that's a shit excuse. I was imagining you on the touchline, wearing your fur-lined coat and those fancy Country boots you liked to wear. You were leaning on the barrier and watching me, no one else, just me. Maybe it was the longing for it to be real and not just in my head that was distracting me.

Whatever the reason, it was 42-6 to them, Swifty crossing in the first five minutes for us, and we were once again about to face a goal line drop out. I'd been caught napping and I had to bat the ball dead in-goal. This was the third set of six we had to defend, and they didn't seem to be tiring. I were on me last legs, hunched over under the sticks trying to catch me breath. Hadn't been this out of breath since that night we had your parent's house to ourselves for the night.

Yozzer drop kicked the ball and the rest of the team ran, well as best they could, as a line. Their fullback caught the ball on the full at halfway and gave a pop pass to a charging forward. He were a big fella and he ran towards our defensive line hard. Skip and Mac wrapped him up, but his momentum took him into the twenty. Thatto didn't do anything silly, so they just crashed the ball up for five tackles then once again dabbed a kick into the in-goal area. Swifty gathered it but was unable to escape as three Crusaders swallowed him up and he's trapped in goal for another goal line drop out. Then the ref blew his whistle, once, twice, then an extended third blast; full time.

Thank God that.

The majority of Phoenix lads fell to the floor as the Crusaders embraced each other in celebration, before coming over and shaking all our hands. I lay on my back on a patch of grass that hadn't been destroyed by studs. All I wanted to do was shower and go home to you. After games like this one, that's all I wanted. We could have got a Chinese, put on some shit Marvel film and cuddled up. But the thought of another lonely night crept across my imagination. Their captain approached me and I got up to shake his hand.

'Unlucky lads, see ya at your place,' he said.

Thatto Heath created the players tunnel and applauded us. We gave them a half-hearted, crestfallen tunnel in return and went into the away changing rooms. You have no idea how losing feels. You've never lost anything. Not even me. I lost you. So I don't know how to tell you how this feels.

'Chin up lads, not what we wanted before the social but let's forget about it, have a couple here then get back to the club,' Skip said, patting each of our backs as we entered the changing room. Damnit, I had forgotten about the social. At least this time I wasn't going to wake you up at five-am stinking of sweat and tequila, requesting sex and then passing out fully clothed. I took off my shirt and threw it into the middle of the room.

'Come on Taz, I know you're annoyed lad but we all have off games,' Mac said to me. I curled my mouth in a small smile, nodded and sat down.

I played like shit today, Shona. I wish you'd stop invading my brain during games. I dropped the first bomb on our own ten metre line and that just set me off. I can't remember the last time I missed so many tackles. At least four of their tries were my fault. I stared at the floor. I hated games like this. Part of me didn't even want to go out now. I just wanted to go home. That sounded so much better right now than trying to act happy.

A pint would sort me out. Always did. I mean, seeing you would have been preferable, but I gotta work with what I got.

I showered with the rest of the lads, dressed in a shirt and club tie which is standard dress for socials, unless a fancy dress has been stated, and went through to the Thatto Heath club house. Again something you never really understood, the whole shirt and tie thing. You'd been with too many footballers I think. They would just wear a polo and then fuck off after.

Suddenly, I had a pint of smooth in my hand.

'Tetley's mate,' Yozzer said.

'Come on pal. We'll have one or two here, back to the club-house, play a little Fuck the Bus and get twated.' Swifty put his hand on my shoulder.

'Might just go home after this one,' I said.

'Don't be like that, mate.'

'Suppose at least I'll get Dickhead of the Day.'

'You know that isn't what it's for.'

'I deserve it.'

I was wrong. Samoa got it for being sidestepped by a fat, forty-year-old prop and falling on his arse. We didn't do Dickhead of the Day until we got back to Sutton though, by which point I'd had two pints and was feeling even shittier, so Yozzer got me to "Fuck the Bus". God, you're going to think we are idiots, but here we go.

It's a moronic card game. Nine cards are set up in a diamond, then the one at the top of the deck is turned over and you basically play higher or lower across the diamond Blockbusters style. If you get it wrong, you shot some port and start again. You're not allowed to stop until you reach the end.

See, moronic.

Eleven shots of port. Eleven. I hate the stuff. But rules are rules. Plus the... seven(?) pints of smooth I'd drank I was pretty smashed. When I eventually reached the end I stood up and punched the air. Then we had a boat race, which Yozzer, Swifty, Samoa, Newbie and I beat Skip, Mac, Carl, Coach and Zack. By now I was well and truly smashed. I bet you're really glad I wasn't coming home to you now.

The taxi picked us up at half ten and before I knew it, I was in the Punch Tarmey, that Irish bar you never liked. I went to the bathroom and returned to the wrong end of the bar. When I realised that the two balding forty-year olds I was stood with weren't my friends, I walked to the other end and found Yozzer and Swifty talking to two girls. I didn't want to cock block them, so I turned to leave, but Yozzer grabbed my arm.

'Girls, this is Taz,' he said, 'Taz, this is Alicia.'

You know what, Shona, this girl was pretty fit. She was small, and so looked up at me through a pair of round glasses. Her hair was long and brown, except for the tips which were dyed blonde. Just like her glasses, her face was also round, and she smiled a calming smile with white teeth. She had this cute little birth mark on her forehead, right by her hairline.

She looked nothing like you. Maybe that's what I liked. For the first time in a long time I wasn't comparing her to you. I had done with every other girl Yozzer introduced me to. But this one, I couldn't compare. I'm not saying she was better looking, I'm not saying you are, I'm saying I couldn't compare.

'Hi,' was all I could muster.

'Hi,' she replied. I couldn't think of anything to say. I was stood there, looking at this girl and my brain couldn't put two words together. Eventually I said. 'Can I get you a drink?'

'Sure, I'd love a gin and tonic.'

We went to the bar together. As we walked, I turned back to look at Yozzer who was giving me the thumbs up. Then he went back to talking to the other girl with Swifty. This wasn't the first girl I'd spoken to since you, but for some reason I was nervous.

'Is Taz your real name?' Alicia asked.

'Nah, my name's Jamie, but everyone just calls me Taz.'

'How come?'

'Well,' I sighed. I couldn't believe I was about to show her my tattoo. 'Because I got this done when I was eighteen.'

Alicia snorted, then put her hand on my arm and gave me a half patronising, half sad smile. 'Oh honey…' pretty much the same reaction you gave. But you know what, I still bloody love my tattoo.

'I know, I was young, I was stupid!' We squeeze ourselves to the bar.

'So you play with those guys?' Alicia asked me.

'Yeah, for Sutton.'

'Your friend was telling me you're the best player on the team.'

'Oh did he?' I had to give Yozzer his dues he was a damn good wingman. I reckon if he spotted you he'd try and hook us up. He was a good mate, our Yozzer.

'Do you think you are?'

'I'm OK,' I said, trying to not to sound too arrogant, but also wanting her to think of me as a decent player.

'I go to watch Saints every now and then. I love it.'

'We're going on Thursday.'

'So am I, with my friend over there. Maybe we'll see you.'

'I hope so. Oh, err hi, can I get a pint of Guinness and a gin and tonic,' I said to the barmaid as she handed change to the guy next to me and nodded.

'Double or single?'

'Double, please,' I replied before Alicia could say anything. So used to you asking for a double every time I just do it out of habit now.

'You didn't have to get me a double.'

'It's not a problem. So what do you do?'

'I'm in admin, I work at a logistics company in town. You?'

'I'm a warehouse assistant for a furniture company.'

We got our drinks and looked to return to our friends, but they had gone. Instead, we eyed up a booth that had been recently abandoned and took a seat. The light above the table gave me more of a look at what Alicia looked like. Her hair was lighter than I had thought and her skin paler. It didn't look like that she was wearing a lot of makeup, which I liked. She had one or two freckles on her cheeks, and I could see the birth mark on her forehead more clearly; it was shaped like a little map of Ireland. Honestly Shona, you would have found her beautiful as well.

'How old are you?' She asked. I was slightly taken aback, not the usual kind of question.

'Twenty-six,' I said.

'You look a little older, I would have said thirty.'

'Is that a good thing or a bad thing?'

'I don't know.' Alicia sipped her drink. 'Just thought you looked older.'

'What about you?'

'Twenty-eight.'

'So you were hoping I was a bit older?'

'No. I don't mind.'

We talked about a lot of things. She had a decent job, better than mine, close to management level, which was kind of impressive. She liked rugby, comic book movies and Phil Collins. She was assertive, maybe because she was older than most of the girls that Yozzer gets us talking to and obviously, I had a couple of years on you. It was her leading the conversation and asking the questions. I liked that, as I was useless around women. You started talking to me, remember. Well, your mate did and she introduced us. Your works do and I had wandered in by mistake and I couldn't think of what to say to you either. It's weird; I didn't mind running at a guy twice my size and taking a big hit but put a beautiful woman in front of me and I suddenly turned into a damn mouse.

As we looked to finish our drinks, Alicia spotted one of her friends over the bar. I couldn't see Yozzer or Swifty anywhere. Goodness knows where they had gone. Alicia's friend beckoned her, and she nodded.

'It was really nice to meet you, Jamie,' she said, turning to look at me. Oh God, this is the bit I was shit at. Making a move. We'd only been speaking for less than an hour, enough time to crack on? What did I do with you? Didn't I try and kiss you and you turned so I got your cheek?

'Yeah, you too,' was all I said. There was a silence that lasted only a few seconds, but to me years passed.

'Maybe I'll see you at the game?' Alicia said.

'Could I get your number? Maybe we could meet up?' Alicia smiled.

'Sure,' she took my phone and entered in her number. 'Have a good night.'

And with that she left. Now I had to find those two idiots. Sod it, I went home instead. I'm not sure why I just wrote all that. Am I trying to make you jealous? Yeah, maybe. Or maybe I just want you to hear about my life. You don't follow us on Instagram anymore, but I still want you to see what I'm doing. And yes, I kind of want you see me flirting with another girl. Maybe it would make you miss me. I wish you did miss me. I miss you.

Jamie

***

Wednesday, May 17th

Weight:	87.2Kgs
Instagram Posts:	Two
Max Bench:	120Kgs
Suicidal Thoughts:	One and a Half
Mental State:	Nervous AF

Dear Shona,

I'm not long back from my date with Alicia and what am I doing? Writing another letter to you. I guess I want you to be the first person I tell. Though even if I send this out I don't suppose you will even read it. It's like the game the other week. I wanted to tell you first. Though tonight, I guess I want to make you a little jealous as well. Remind you what it's like to be with me.

To be honest I wasn't expecting Alicia to even text back, let alone to get the date with her. You know me, bloody paranoid about getting a response. Checking my phone every thirty seconds. But we had chatted all week. I texted Sunday evening, she replied and since then it'd been non-stop. And I've liked it. Though we said we might meet up at the Saints game on Thursday, *she* asked *me* out. How in the Hell did that happen? We had spoken about the food we liked, I said Mr Chan's Chinese was mint, so she said we should go. Together.

So, we did.

I was so nervous. As nervous as I was before our first date. Remember that? Saints V Wigan and I got us seats on the half-way line. I think I was genuinely sweating as I walked towards the restaurant. All kinds of thoughts were sweeping through my head. First and foremost, was she actually going to be there when I showed up? Was my hair looking good? It hadn't really behaved itself after I got out of the shower. What if I said something stupid? What if I accidentally insulted her? Maybe she was the leader of a cult and was actually just recruiting me. What if this was a joke, set up by Yozzer, and I was about to turn the corner to see him and Swifty laughing at me. Nah, he wasn't that much of a twat, even if he did get me to talk about our sex life. Again, I'm sorry.

When I did turn the corner, to my upmost relief, Alicia was standing outside going through her phone. She looked really classy, like. She had nice heeled boots on, blue jeans and a leather jacket. This did remind me of you and your fashion sense. Her hair was tied up off her face and I could see the cute Ireland birth mark. I felt totally underdressed now in an old pair of skinny jeans, a plain black polo shirt and a knock-off Barbour jacket.

'Hey you,' she said, looking up from her phone.

'Hiya love, you all right?' I replied as I went for a hug.

'Aye, I'm grand,' Alicia kissed my cheek. A sudden pang of excitement rushed over my body.

'Shall we? I'm starving,' I ushered her towards the door. She smiled and nodded.

'Me too, I've barely eaten all day!'

Mr Chan put us on a cosy table away from the kitchen. I ordered a bottle of Tiger beer and Alicia got a gin and tonic as she looked through the wine menu. I picked up the food menu and plucked a prawn cracker out of the basket in the middle of the table. You used to always eat pretty much all of them so

I guess now I'm on my guard.

'Shall we get a bottle?' Alicia asked.

'I don't mind,' I said, quickly swallowing the partial cracker in my mouth, causing me to cough and grab my beer. Alicia laughed.

'You all right there, petal?'

'Oh aye, I'm grand!' I swig from the bottle again.

'So, wine?' She repeated.

'Yeah, go on, why not.'

'Do you care what it is?'

'Not at all,' I used a napkin to dab around my mouth, trying, and most likely failing, to come across nonchalant. It was times like now I wish I'd listened to all the times you tried to educate me on wine.

When the waiter came over, I ordered shredded chicken to start and sweet and sour pork for main. She ordered chilli prawns and then chicken in black bean sauce. We decided to split an order of fried rice and Alicia ordered a wine from the menu; a Sauv Blanc I think. Whatever it was, it was bloody lovely. One thing you have in common with her is your wine taste. We'd drank a glass each by the time our starters arrived. I was so nervous. Under the table, I could feel my leg twitching, up and down, like a pneumatic drill in that way that would always make you slap my knee to stop. I wonder how you would react now knowing that it's anxiety that causes it. Probably still the same.

'Do you work out, Jamie?' Alicia started the conversation, as she had done every time.

'Yeah, I go to Olympia, do you know it?'

Alicia shook her head. 'I can't say I've heard of it.'

'It's a little out of town, but I like it.'

'How often do you go?'

'Pretty much every day,' I said, dipping a piece of chicken in sweet chilli sauce.

'I keep meaning to re-join DW. I need to get back,' Alicia said.

'Oh behave, like heckers you do!'

'You're just being sweet,' Alicia continued, 'but I do. Getting too much junk in the trunk!'

I shrugged. I didn't want to be that guy who just rained compliments on her, she'd never respect me if I did. I know I used to do it you far too often.

When our mains arrived, we ordered a second bottle of wine. It was going down a little too quick. Though it was loosening me up. I felt my body literally untighten and I slipped forward a little in my chair. I could even feel myself smiling. Alicia was great she really was. The conversation was flowing, I even made a couple of jokes that she laughed at. I know right, me being funny, I bet you don't believe it. Well to be fair, they weren't funny, was she flirting with me? Her eyes sparkled through her glasses when she laughed, and I got a warm breeze of excitement every time. She told me she had just bought her own house, she had two cats and she got to travel to Europe every now and then for work.

'So where do you go?' I asked.

'Sweden, mostly. Occasionally Norway, Denmark, a lot of work in Scandinavia really.'

'That's pretty cool!'

'It's even better work pay for it,' she winks at me. There's that breeze again.

'Come on then, what's your favourite place?' I continued to

probe. I was a little proud of myself, I was actually keeping the conversation moving. I don't really like talking about myself, unless it was about rugby league, you know that, so it was nice to hear about her.

'I think Sweden. It's a beautiful country over there. Have you ever been?'

'I've barely left the UK,' I said.

'Seriously?'

'OK, no that's a lie, I've been to Ireland on tour, and France once or twice.'

'But never further afield?'

'Nope.'

'How come?'

'Just never got around to it. Money and work. The usual excuses.'

'You're right, they are excuses. You need to have a holiday at least! See a bit of the world.'

'Me mate were trying to get us tickets for the Catalans game at the weekend,' I said.

'Well there you go! You get your rugby and away for a bit!'

'Aint heard nothing though, so God knows if he's sorted it.'

'If he doesn't then you need to get away somewhere, just relax.'

She was right. I hadn't had a proper holiday in my years, and it catches up with you, I mean we never went anywhere. Rugby is great and all that, but sometimes you just need to relax. Alicia sipped her wine and continued.

'I lived for six months in Canada when I was twenty-one.'

'Really? Doing what?' I was impressed.

'Ski season. I was in Banff, have you heard of it?'

I shook my head.

'It's beautiful over there, and party central. Best six months of my life, bar none.'

I was fascinated by her. She told me all about her time in Canada, the wildlife she saw, trips to Vancouver and Edmonton. She told me how she thought she'd broken her leg skiing, but it was just a sprain. She told me about the friends she'd made and ski jobs she did. Canada sounded amazing, we should have gone when we had the chance to holiday together.

Then we did the bill dance.

'Do you want me to get half?' she asked. I shook my head.

'No honestly, this is on me.'

'Really? I feel bad, at least let me give you some money?'

'I tell you what,' I said, taking my bank card out of my wallet and hanging it to the waiter, 'you can treat me, next time you see me.'

Alicia bit her lower lip.

There it was again, that sudden rush of warmth.

'Yeah, OK. I'd love to see you again,' she said.

We got up and left the restaurant together and began walking through town.

'Where do you live?' she asked.

'In town, above the Golden Dragon?'

'Oh yeah, I know where you mean.'

'I'd invite you round for a drink or something, but my flat is a tip.'

'I'm not coming home with you tonight, Jamie,' Alicia nudged me with her shoulder. 'Besides, I have work tomorrow, so I'd better get a taxi.'

'I'll walk you to the rank.'

'You don't have to do that.'

'It's fine, there's one just around the corner,' I pointed down the street. Then I returned my hand into my pocket. Suddenly, Alicia threaded her arm through mine.

'You're sweet.'

The taxi rank was around the next corner. Alicia leaned into the window to ask if the driver could take her to her house in Eccleston. She turned around to face me and looked up at me. The pang of warm excitement had been replaced with one of nerves. In my stomach, there weren't only butterflies, but any other winged creatures you could think of flapping around, bouncing against the inside of my abbs.

'I had a lovely night,' she said. I swallowed. Hard.

'Me too. Text me and let me know you get home?'

'Yeah, I will,' she nodded. Her eyes were still locked with mine. Alicia bit her lower lip again and I thought sod it. I went in for the kiss.

Her lips moved in motion with mine. Her hand found the back of my head and both of mine rested gently on her hips. Her tongue slipped into my mouth and massaged itself softly against mine. My stomach was suddenly calm.

'Good night,' Alicia said, pulling her face from mine and climbing into the taxi. I watched it drive off around the corner, before I punched the air.

'Come on!' I yelled.

I'm sorry if this letter is coming across a bit more aggressive or something. After writing this it does make me resent you a little. Why did you want to throw that away? And how come you and I never did on go holiday? We spoke about it loads but we never did. Paris, Venice, Barcelona, all these romantic spots but nothing ever came of it. Was that my fault? It's just something that never really materialised. Money, time, whatever the reason it just didn't happen. Just think how nice it would have been if we had actually gone somewhere better than Scarborough or the Fylde Coast. But tonight Shona, Oh God I finally had something to smile about. I just hope you can be happy for me, at least.

Jamie.

***

St Helens, May 19th

Hours worked:	Thirty-eight and a half
Gym Sessions:	Five
Mood:	Chilled
Suicidal Thoughts:	A Half
Arm workouts:	Three
Leg Workouts:	Not enough

Dear Shona

Did we ever contemplate going to Perpignan together to go and watch Saints v Catalan? I can't remember if that ever fell into any of our plans. I just got thinking about it after the last letter I wrote you. I'm sure I must have suggested it at some point. I spoke about going there for years. Well, I was just chilling out, feet up, eating pasta and watching *Comedy Central*, a relaxed Friday night, when my phone went off. I wiped my hand on my shirt, reached over, read the word 'Yozzer' on the screen, then swiped to answer.

'Hey mate,' I said.

'You packed?' Yozzer asked.

'What?'

'Plane leaves from John Lennon at ten tomorrow.'

'Bloody Hell, pal. You left it a bit last minute didn't you?'

'That's how you get it cheap,' Yozzer said, 'anyway, get your shit together and you can crash at mine. Oh and get Swifty on your way. I'm gonna email you the game ticket as well, don't need to print it or nothing. We'll sort the money when you get here.'

'Erm, yeah OK.'

'Exactly! You don't sound excited mate, we've been meaning to do this for years.'

'Course I'm excited, Just last minute, innit?'

'Good, right I'll see you in a bit pal.'

That was the thing about Yozzer, he always did everything last minute. You'd call it spontaneous; I'd call it unorganised. I dragged myself off the sofa, tossing the half-eaten pasta in the bin. Through in my bedroom I emptied my rucksack, throwing boots and deep heat onto my bed. I was just about to start folding up a spare t-shirt and grab some undies and socks when my phone went off. It was a WhatsApp message from Yozzer.

'Grab us a Big Mac on your way pal.'

He so cheeky.

I packed quickly, grabbed my passport from my bedside table, messaged Swifty to say I was on my way and left. Swifty's weren't far from me; only about five minutes. I picked him up and went to the nearest Maccy Ds, the one a few streets over from yours. I got an overwhelming urge to drive over but controlled myself. Besides, I was thinking about someone else as well as you now. At Maccys we ordered two Big Macs and a double cheeseburger for Swifty, three large cokes and three large chips. I miss ordering you your McChicken sandwich. What a thing to miss, eh? Then we headed over to Yozzer's.

'Did you get us a Big Mac?'

'Yes, I got you a bloody Big Mac.'

'Good lad. Taxi is gonna get us at seven tomorrow. Who wants the sofa bed and who wants the blow-up mattress?'

'I don't mind,' Swifty said, tucking into his chips as we sat around Yozzer's kitchen table.

'Go on, I'll have the air bed pal, you had it last time,' I said. I poured my chips into the lid of my Big Mac, a quirk you never got your head around.

'Cheers, pal.'

'So, game kicks off at six local time, afterwards we can get on the piss. Fly back Sunday. Got us in at hotel in Perpignan, two single beds and a fold out.'

'Shotgun,' Swifty and I said in unison.

'You can't call shotgun now.'

'Why not?' I asked.

'Standard shotgun rules,' Yozzer explained, 'You have to be in view of the bed to call shotgun on it.'

'Since when?'

'Since always. You gotta be able to see what it is you're calling shotgun on.'

'He's right,' Swifty said.

'See!'

'OK. Well, I guess whoever gets in the room first gets the beds.'

'I guess so. Beer?' Yozzer got up and threw the empty Big Mac box in the bin. He'd hardly touched his coke. Then he went to the fridge and pulled out a bottle of Bud.

'I'm pretty beat mate, might just go to bed,' Swifty said. I look over at him as it's only nine thirty.

'Seriously?'

'Yeah, I'm pretty tired. Long week.'

'You work in admin!'

Swifty shrugged and finished the rest of his burger. He'd taken out the gherkin and put it in the empty chip carton, as he'd eaten them first, as he always does. He must have been over working himself, as he's been saying he's been tired a lot recently. Poor bastard does work hard.

'Soft arse,' Yozzer said. 'Did you take that bird out then Taz?'

I smiled. I had wanted an excuse to talk about my date with Alicia.

'Yeah mate, I did.'

'Well? What happened? Snog her? Shag her?'

'Bloody hell, Yozzer, not all of us shag on the first date.'

'Or if you're Swifty, shag on any date,' Yozzer joked. Swifty smiled, but I could tell that hit a little close to home.

'Leave him alone,' I said.

'He knows I'm playing. Didn't you take a bird out this week and all?'

'Sheila, yeah. She was nice.'

'Tell me you snogged her, at least.'

'Well…'

'Fuck's sake man!'

'I don't kiss on the first date!'

'That's a load of toss! ALWAYS kiss on the first date!'

Swifty shrugged again. Yozzer had placed a Budweiser in front of him and he reluctantly took a swig. There was a beer in front of me as well, which I gulped down. Salty food always made me thirsty.

'What about you then, pal?' I asked Yozzer.

'What about me?'

'Birds?'

'I shagged Natalie again.'

I sighed and rubbed my face with both hands.

'Oh not this again. Have you two actually been on a date?'

'Yozzer doesn't date,' Swifty said, peeling the label of his beer bottle.

'We're mates, friends. With benefits. And don't lewk at me like that, it were her idea. She don't want a relationship, neither do I, we both like sex. Everyone's happy.

'And you sleep with other people?'

'Well yeah, or that would be a relationship.'

'Do you not get jealous?' Swifty asked.

'To be honest pal, I don't ask. I'd rather not think about it to be honest.'

'So you do get jealous?'

'Nah, it aint like that.'

'I dunno pal, I think someone went to Oz and got a heart,' Swifty said.

'Sod off, Swifty!'

Swifty smiled to himself as he continued to pick at the label on the bottle. I shook my head. I'd started thinking about Alicia again. She'd messaged me earlier but I hadn't replied. I didn't want to seem too eager. But in reality, I was. The date had been awesome, the kiss had been awesome, and so were she. I looked over at Swifty, still peeling the label. He did look pretty tired.

It got me thinking about our first date. That Saints Wigan game. Twenty-two-twelve I think it finished. You had a chicken pie and a bottle of Crabbies at half time. I had a meat pie and Crabbies as well. Then drinks at somewhere in town. I can't remember where it was though, somewhere you frequent and somewhere I felt a little out of place in. But I went there cause I fancied you that much. And we definitely kissed, definitely. One of the best kisses of my life Shona. I remember how soft your lips felt and how gently your tongue massaged against mine. Damn, what a kiss. I won't be forgetting that one in a while. Will you?

Jamie.

***

Perpignan, May 20th

Hours slept:	Not Enough
Flight Time:	Two Hours
Saints fans on the Plane:	Loads
Overpriced Cans Drunk:	Three
Toilet Trips:	Four
Times Told to Behave:	Three

Dear Shona,

Yozzer had booked us an absolute shit hole for the one night we were staying in Perpignan. I mean, the whole weekend was gonna cost about a hundred-and-fifty quid, not including food and drink, so we couldn't really complain. But we did. Numerous times. It's certainly not the kind of hotel I'd want to take you to. I'd want a balcony and a view of the castle that I could kiss you in front of. Not stained walls and a view of some French woman hanging out her washing.

'Well you cunts can sort it next time,' Yozzer had said. The room was tiny. The two single beds looked like the mattresses hadn't been changed in twenty years and the fold out… well the less said about that the better. There were a shower and a toilet and a sink in the bathroom and that was it. The only redeeming feature was we weren't far from the middle of Perpignan, so getting on the piss after the game was going to be a lot easier. Swifty took the foldout after losing at rock paper scissors. They'd let us check in a little earlier which was nice of them, though the owners spoke as much English as we did French.

'Where good, drink and food?' I asked. I don't know why, but for someone reason when I speak to foreign people I suddenly act like I'm speaking to a two-year-old. It's so condescending, but I suppose they don't realise that. You took GCSE French, shame we didn't have you there to translate.

'Café La Poste,' they said, along with a sentence I can't for the life of me attempt to say nor remember to be fair. In one ear and out the other with French. Swifty, Yozzer and I were all in our Saints shirts, so I guess that's why we got directed to the café-bar La Poste, as once we got there around one it was crawling with St Helens fans. We spotted Mac and Skip through the crowds, so went to join them.

'Hey up, lads,' Mac said, 'how do?'

'All good pal,' Yozzer said, 'you need a beer?'

'We're good mate, just got a round in.'

Yozzer and I went to the bar and Swifty stayed with Mac and Skip. We said hello to a couple of fans that we see regularly at home games as we squeezed through to the front. There was a very attractive blonde girl working behind the bar and, of course, Yozzer eyed her up straight away.

'Bonjour,' he said as she walked past, serving a couple of older gents in the latest away shirts at the end of the bar. She gave a short smile, clearly too busy and more than likely far to used to dickheads like Yozzer hitting on her whilst she is trying to work. You'd hate Yozzer after a few drinks.

'You're a knobhead,' I said.

'What do you reckon her name is?'

'I don't know! Michelle, that's a French name, innit?'

'I reckon it's Natasha,' Yozzer pondered, watching the poor girl serve the two lads that were before us. Out the front, I could hear a chorus of *When the Saints go Marching In* starting up.

'Just order the beers pal and let's get outside!'

'Bonjour, three large bierres, ci-vous plait,' Yozzer said, still with his thick Merseyside accent. Damn, we really could have done with you.

'Did you even pass French?'

'Didn't take it, did Spanish.'

'You can tell,' I said, pulling out my phone. As I looked through Instagram, seeing that Saints had put up a video of the fans out the front of the very bar we were in, I got a message from Alicia.

'Hey you, are you around tonight? Me and the girls are out for drinks if you and your mates wanted to meet up? Xxx'

'That your bird?' Yozzer asked, handing me a pint of Heineken.

'One date mate, hardly my bird!'

'Date went well though, yeah?'

'Yeah, it did mate. Just asking if we are out tonight.'

'Shame, her mates looked fit.'

'Just gimme me pint!'

'Let's get this down Swify's neck, he seems a little quiet!'

'It's the women mate,' I took a large swig of my beer as Yozzer still carried his and Swify's, 'he does get pissed about and he just wants to meet someone.'

'He needs to relax.'

'Yeah, I know mate, this weekend will help him forget about those bitches that have been using him!'

'He dunt half know how to pick 'em, does he?'

We took the beers back and started to get on it. The chanting and singing were becoming louder and the atmosphere was mint. Honestly, you'd have absolutely loved it here. Kick off weren't until six so we had loads of time. After a few at La Poste we looked at moving on. Mac had been to Catalans before.

'We'll get the bus, pal, free with your ticket and takes you from 'ere to right out-front o' stadium!' he said, his accent getting even thicker, as it always did, as he got pissed. So we followed him and Skip to a bus stop about two minutes from the café, hopped on, and rode it to the stadium.

The Stade de Gilbert Brutus was decent. I'd seen it on telly before, but it's never the same as actually seeing it. All the Saints fans would be behind the posts, but we had plenty of time before kick-off so we once again followed Mac and Skip. They took us to a bar on the corner, which was once again teaming with St Helens fans. I think I saw a couple of your friends. It must have been, because when they noticed me they quickly moved away.

'This is where all the away fans come,' Skip said, 'here y'are, I'll get these in boys, don't worry, no point us all going bar.'

So we waited out the front and joined in with more singing, this time chanting along to how much we hated Wigan. Suddenly, the crowd started booing.

'What's going on?' Swifty asked, straining his neck.

'Dunno pal,' I said, struggling to see over the crowd.

'It's some dickhead in a Wigan shirt!' Mac shouted. He was on a step, so could see a little better and pointed over the heads.

'What?' Yozzer asked.

'Some bellend over there is wearing a scummy Wigan shirt, get it off him! Wanker, Wanker!' Mac started chanting and thrusting a finger in the Wigan fan's direction as the crowd started joining in. Swifty, Yozzer and I started chanting along with them as Skip brought out five Heinekens in a branded drinks tray.

'Wanker, wanker, wanker!'

The bloke had his arms in the air. He knew what he was doing. He was just trying to rile us up. To be fair it was working. Then the chanting turned into cheers. The bloke's mates had taken the shirt off him and it got passed around the crowd. The bloke didn't seem bothered. Probably all part of it.

'Burn it!' Mac yelled, cupping his hand around his mouth!

'Yeah, burn that shite!' Someone else yelled. I quickly had my phone out, along with Yozzer, ready to film. A couple of lads grabbed the shirt and a space cleared in front of him. After a few attempts with a dodgy lighter, the red shirt set alight. Yes I know what you're thinking 'so immature.' But you know you would have been filming it as well.

The cheer from the crowd was like a Saints try. Another rendition of *Saints go Marching In* started up as fists flew in the air and beer sprayed everywhere. Mac was like a ring leader, putting all his might into singing. He was a diehard fan, supported the Saints all his life. On the floor just a few feet away from us the ritualistic burning of the Wigan shirt was coming to an end. The material smouldered on the concrete.

We had a few more before moving on to the stadium. By this point, I was pretty smashed. So were the others. We still had half an hour so thought best to get a beer in the stadium, find our seats and prepare ourselves. Unfortunately, it wasn't quite that simple.

Catalan Dragons have this weird concept. You have to buy tokens from a stand first, then use these tokens at the bars and food vans. It was one euro for one token, so I bought twenty. It was then five tokens at the bar for a pint of beer, Carlsberg

I think, but I can't be sure, I was hammered. I didn't care by this point though. This took a little longer than intended and we found our seats behind the sticks just as the teams were coming out for the game.

The stand was cool, quite steep so good views all around. I'm sorry though, I can't remember the score. It was about eighteen-ten to them at half time, but I had three more beers at the break and barely remember the rest of the game. All I can remember from the game was that we lost. Bloody typical. All that way and we lost.

We got the bus back to the middle of town and found a pizzeria that didn't look too busy. La Roma, I think it was called. Whatever it was, I had calamari for a starter and then a huge pepperoni and salami pizza. That sobered me up a little, so we got a big cheese board between us for desert. Now that's something you did teach me about; cheese. Then, I had a panic.

I hadn't messaged Alicia back. I know, I know, not the end of the world, but you know how neurotic I am

Now I had to attempt to reply, pissed off my face. I sent her the following message:

'Heyyy!11 Sory, Im france watching Saints! We lost ☹ you hving a good nite?'

We went for a wander and found an Irish bar along from a couple of cocktail bars. We looked set for the evening. They did Guinness, so I was happy. We sat outside, since it was still pretty warm.

'After these, can we check out that cocktail bar?' Yozzer asked, clumsily looking over his shoulder at a group of attractive women sat under the umbrellas of the nearby cocktail place.

'Whatever mate,' I said, 'Swift, Swifty, oi, you keen?' Swifty was clutching his pint like a two-year-old clutching their favourite teddy bear.

'Huh, wha?'

'After these, cocktails over, over…' Yozzer hiccoughed, 'over there.'

'I'm smashed mate.'

'Yeah, but cocktails, pal. And there's some birds,' Yozzer said.

'Oh, speaking of birds,' I pulled out my phone.

'Put that damn phone away!' Yozzer reached out and I moved it from his grasping hands.

'Wait, let me, let me just check,' I too hiccoughed.

'No! Mate, you're with the lads, you know the rules!'

There was a message from Alicia, but I couldn't read it properly. I think it said something along the lines of saying that she was jealous I was here and that she hoped I was having a good time. And then there was a picture of her. A selfie, in her mirror, of her in a red dress and her leather jacket. Damn, she looked good. I tried to compose myself to reply, but instead I wrote the following:

'You look fit as fuck, I've been thinking of you xxXx.'

I would regret that the next morning, but in my drunken state, I didn't care. You remember all those drunken flirty messages when we were first dating? Yeah, I haven't changed. Yozzer still had his hand out trying to get my phone.

'Give me the damn thing.'

I handed it to him. He couldn't get into it anyway as he didn't know my passcode. But we had a rule. Text a bird on lad's night, lose your phone. Like you women try and stop each other texting lads.

'I might go back, I'm smashed,' Swifty said again, not looking up and swaying.

'Mate, no! Cocktails, and birds! Don't be a pussy!' Yozzer said and he raised the three-quarters full glass of Guinness, knocked his head back and downed it.

'Fuck it!' I said and followed suit.

'I'm smashed,' Swifty said for a third time.

'Leave that then mate and let's have some cocktails!'

We stumbled into the next bar. They were clearly a lot more lapse about serving drunkards in France, as they had no problem making us three Long Island Iced Teas. Smashed off our faces and we ordered the strongest cocktail on the menu. Yeah, I know, dickheads.

Yozzer lead the way to the girls and started chatting them up. I wish I had his confidence I really do. Swifty once again hugged his drink and I just watched Yozzer work his magic. Pissed, he still had a certain charm. Maybe they were drunk as well. I looked back at Swifty. He was asleep, his head on the table. I motioned towards him and Yozzer rolled his eyes.

'Here,' he said, handing me my phone, 'take him back and I'll see you back at the hotel. I woke Swifty up picked him off his chair. My arm around him, we walked in a zig-zag towards the hotel.

'I want a kebab,' Swifty said.

'Yeah, actually so do I.'

I tell you, French kebabs were good. I mean really good. It hit the spot like Phil Taylor chucking arrows. We couldn't carry them, far too drunk, so we sat in the window of the kebab shop and scoffed them down, making a right mess. Again, made me miss ordering your usual. Chicken nuggets and chips with a shit ton of mayonnaise, I remember. Then we set off.

Swifty's kebab lasted about a hundred yards before he threw up in a bush.

'All right pal, let's just get you back,' I reassured him, patting his back.

In the hotel, he spent half an hour with his head in the toilet. I had time to check my phone. No message from Alicia. Maybe she'd hooked up with some bloke. Damn, I was even more neurotic when I was pissed and I hated it. I checked her Instagram. Just one picture of her and three other girls was up. I smiled. I was being silly, she weren't that type of girl. She just liked going out with her mates. She weren't into hooking up with lads on nights out. I was surprised at myself. Usually I'd be a lot more paranoid than this that maybe she would be. But there were something about Alicia that even being so far from her, I still felt calm. Why am I telling you this, I'm saying she makes me feel calm and I'm still writing to my damn ex-girlfriend. Wish you'd get out of my head. Swifty came out of the bathroom.

'I'm sorry mate,' he said, wiping his mouth.

'Don't worry mate, I couldn't be arsed with wingmanning Yozzer anyway.'

'You can go back out, don't worry about me,' Swifty flopped onto the pull out and curled up under the covers.

'Honestly, I'm happier back here, You all right mate?'

'I'm OK now. Can I ask you something?'

'Course mate, what's up?'

'Just you though, not Yozzer.'

'He's out with some birds.'

'OK, cool. Is there summet wrong with me? Like why girls don't wanna be more than friends with me?'

I was taken aback. I wasn't expecting that from him. For a few seconds I was quiet before I responded.

'No mate. No, of course there's nothing wrong with you.'

'I just don't get it.'

'You pick the wrong ones. You pick girls that will walk all over you, use you and date assholes.'

'Why do they date assholes, though? Why not us nice guys.'

I suddenly thought about Alicia. She was into nice guys, I think.

'I don't know mate. I honestly don't know. Just get some sleep, don't worry about that now. You'll meet someone soon enough.'

'Did I tell you I had trials at Saints?'

'Erm, I think you mentioned it once.'

'I was good man. I played for Leigh reserves; did I tell you that?'

'No, I never knew that,' I said, suddenly a lot more interested. Did you know Swifty played reserve grade rugby? That's pretty impressive, especially at Leigh.

'Yeah, when I was eighteen. Then I broke my leg.'

'Shit, really? How'd that happen.'

'No one's fault, my leg got caught and it snapped. Couldn't play for two years.'

'Fucking Hell Swifty. No you never told me this.'

'I was about to break into their first team I was well. I was weeks away from a pro contract.'

'They still didn't think to give it you anyway?'

'That sort of injury, nah. You never get back to your best.'

There was silence between us. I'd never heard Swifty open up to me like that before. See, the thing is Shona with professional

72

rugby, you get one shot. They either sign you, or they won't. And if you bust yourself up like that, they aren't going to give you shit. Why would they? Too big a risk. I suppose I could empathise with Swifty, what with all my golf stuff. But damn, I didn't realise he had his dreams crushed like that. Can you imagine that? Imagine everything you want taken away in the blink of eye, because of something that wasn't your fault.

Kind of like us.

I looked over at Swifty. His eyes were closed. 'Night mate,' I said.

'Night mate, thanks mate,' Swifty said, turning over.

'Night mate,' I said again. Still smashed, clearly. . I led back in the shitty single bed and thought about Alicia as I drifted off to sleep. And you. But this Alicia, she was something else. Totally different to you Shona, in every way. Maybe that's why I want to tell you about her. Maybe that's why I think about you both. Maybe this girl will finally get you out of my head. Maybe it'll be her I'm writing letters to. Or maybe I won't ever have to write a letter again soon. Have I said this to you already? Damn, it's the next day and I'm back in England but maybe I'm still drunk. Sorry if I have already said it. I still kind of miss you.

Jamie.

***

St Helens v Leeds Rhinos, Totally Wicked Stadium, May 27th

Pints Drunk:	Five
Minutes at the gym:	Fifty-seven
Max Deadlift:	Still Two-Hundred
Minutes on Cardio:	Five
Suicidal Thoughts:	None
Texts to Alicia:	All Week

Dear Shona,

We went to another game later in the week this time against the Rhinos. Saints were twelve-nil up against Leeds twenty minutes into the first half.

'So, have you shagged her yet?' Yozzer asked me

'I aint telling you that,' I said, sipping John Smiths from a plastic glass. Yozzer, Swifty and I were in the stands behind the sticks that Leeds were attacking, just to the left of the uprights, leaning on one of the metal rails. You hated standing for games, but we love it.

'That's a no,' Yozzer said.

'OK, if you must know, yeah, I shagged her,' I said.

'I knew it,' Swifty said.

'What were she like?' Yozzer asked.

'Come on pal!' I said, taking another swig of smooth.

'Oh come on, when you shagged Shona you wouldn't shut up about it for weeks after!'

'Yeah, well Alicia, Alicia is different mate.'

Yozzer and Swifty look at each other. I try to ignore the sly smile they give each other and watch the game. Saints were camped in Leed's half; another try seemed inevitable.

'Do you love her?' Swifty asked. I take another swig of beer.

'I've only known her two weeks.'

'It don't take long, pal, trust me, love is a drug.'

'Love aint a drug, pal,' Yozzer said, 'it's a fucking mental illness.'

'Ignore him, he hasn't had a relationship last more than a week!'

'Look, I like her, yeah, I do. A lot, to be fair.'

'Get out now then,' Yozzer added, 'oh come on ref, get them onside, for God's sake!'

The game on the field had gone a little dry, both defences were holding firm. Hopefully the second half would pick up and we'd get a bit of excitement. Apart from Wigan, Leeds were the only team I hated, and I mean really hated, losing to. No one likes Leeds.

'Right lads, I'll be back in a minute, get in the bogs before the half time rush,' Yozzer said, checking his watch. The countdown clock below the big screen in the far corner of the stadium indicated that only eight minutes of the half was left. Yozzer downed the rest of the beer from his plastic glass, then sidled his way through the crowd to the stairs. Swifty shifted along the rail to fill the gap Yozzer had left.

'So what about you mate?' I asked him.

'What d'ya mean?'

'Ladies, like what's going on, still talking to that Sheila bird?'

'She said she just wants to be friend,' Swifty said, not even looking at me as he uttered the words, just looking out at the game playing out in front of us and sipping his beer.

'Seriously?'

'Yep.'

'I'm sorry mate, you really liked her, didn't you?'

'Yep.'

'Did she give you any other reason.'

'"You're a really nice guy, Dan, but I just don't feel it, but I still wanna be friends."'

'Never thought I'd say this, but maybe you are being too nice.'

'Maybe.'

We stood in silence as a rendition of 'When the Saints go Marching in' filled the stadium.

'I mean it mate,' I said, 'You do everything for these women, they don't appreciate you, you take them out, you pay for everything.'

Suddenly, Yozzer appeared next to us, sniffing loudly. 'We talking about Swifty's love life now?'

'Yes,' I said, and then 'oh for fuck's sake, Yozzer, wipe your nose!' There was a small smatter of white powder around his nostril, which Yozzer quickly wiped away with the back of his hand.

'Bloody hell, Yozzer, you're gonna get us banned from here, I swear!'

'Relax, that's why I go before half time. Anyway, Taz is right pal, you need to be an asshole!'

'No, Swifty, don't be an asshole, just grow a pair and stop doing everything for these women. How many are you actually still friends with?'

'Kate. Kate messaged me the other night.'

'Kate?' Yozzer exclaimed, 'she hasn't spoken to you in two months and the first thing she asks for is a lift back from Liverpool at two am!'

'And did you go?' I asked.

'Of course he did! Look at me Swifty, am I nice to girls?'

'No, you're a cunt.'

'Exactly, and when did I last have a shag?'

'Do I want to know the answer?'

'An hour before you guys came over. Look at Taz, he's half a cunt, so he has half as much sex as me.'

'Hey!'

'But you, you buy them stuff, and treat them nice, and they walk all over you, get what they can and toss ya aside, before you get anywhere near a shag.'

'I want more than that, though,' Swifty said.

'Ignore him, that's the Charlie talking. Don't change you, just don't be such a pushover, you know?' I tell him. Around us, the crowd started counting down to halftime.

Jamie

***

Ullswater, Cumbria, June 11th

Miles Driven: 105
Convenience Breaks: 2
Number of Times we Sang 500 Miles: 3
Coffees Drunk: 5
Suicidal Thoughts: 0
Times Alicia's Hand Found My Groin: 4

Dear Shona,

I know I haven't written in a while. But things have been good. Really good. Alicia and I have started dating properly now. I told her about my depression up front. She understands. She said she gets it. I got a strange feeling that if I had found out about it earlier maybe it could have saved us.

I'm away for the weekend with Alicia and she has gone to sleep. But I'm still wide awake. I'm away in the Lakes, with a gorgeous girl and all I want to do is tell you about it. I know I shouldn't be writing this letter. Yes, I'm here with Alicia, but I guess, maybe I wish it was you asleep in that bed instead? Is that bad to say whilst my new girl is a few metres away? I was hoping she would get you out of my head. She has done for a couple of weeks. But for some reason, you've walked back in.

Anyway, there was no game this weekend, so Alicia and I had decided to get away from St Helens for a night. She sorted it, she had found some deal on Groupon or something that gave us a cheap hotel, right by one of the lakes in the Lake District. I had never been up there before, but Alicia told me how nice it was. I was so happy, for once I couldn't keep the smile off my face. I hadn't smiled this much since you

The drive up from St Helens to Cumbria was so nice. The sun was beating down, we had classic rock songs blasting out of the stereo and the windows of my Capri were down letting the cool air blow through the car.

The drive itself took over two hours. It should have taken less, but my phone lost signal the moment we got to Ullswater and the Sat Nav app crashed out on us ('It's left here, I'm telling you it's left, left! Oh shit, should have turned right, sorry!'). But neither of us cared. Instead, we just laughed when I ended up down a dirt track and had to reverse half a mile.

The hotel was pretty swish, I had to admit. The girl had done good, even you'd be impressed. It was a regency house. Called the MacDonald Leeming house. We parked around the front and I grabbed our suitcases. I had been surprised at the size of hers when I picked her up, just a small one the same size as my duffel bag. She wasn't one of these girls who needed a big suitcase for one night away, to pack every single hair product and dress into. It was one of the things I liked about her.

We checked in and were shown up to her room. Man, I had to get a Groupon account if this is the kind of last-minute deals you could get. It was proper posh, I tell thee. The ceilings were high and there were busts of Roman senates in little alcoves. We took a wide, red carpeted staircase up to the first floor and found our room easily. Alicia unlocked it and we entered.

'Jesus,' I muttered.

'Nice, eh?'

'Babe, it's proper lush!' Yes, I called her babe.

There was a king bed against one of the walls, with ample room on either side to get changed. A purple tartan style runner hung over the white bedsheets. Opposite the bed was a desk, with a TV on the wall and mini-bar. The room had an en-suite, complete with a shower-over-bath, toilet, sink, and even one of those lady sink things. You know, the one where you wash your arse? I'll be damned if I can remember what they are called.

'Babe, this is posh as they come,' I said, coming out of the bathroom.

'I knew you'd like it,' Alicia said, wrapping her arms around my waist.

'Yeah, I do.'

'So, we get dinner with this deal, we got a table at half seven. We could go for a walk through the fells before then.'

'I can think of something else I'd rather do,' I said, kissing Alicia passionately on her lips.

'Mm, OK, but then we are going exploring!'

We made love for about an hour. I'll spare you the details. Afterwards, I took a shower, it was a better work out then eighty minutes on the pitch, I swear. I washed my hair, lathered my body and popped an annoying spot that had appeared on my arm, right by my *Taz of Tasmania* tattoo. The testosterone was making me break out a little; a frustrating side effect. On the plus side, I looked in the mirror and saw a better, more toned body looking back at me. I smiled, as I knew Alicia liked it as well. Feeling her hands run all over it and see her look of longing at me made me feel so good about myself. I grabbed a towel, dried myself and put on a pair of Oddballs and jogging pants.

Alicia was on the balcony, looking out on the gorgeous views of the Cumbrian Fells and the lake. She had grabbed my Phoenix training shirt and put it on, along with a pair of plain white panties. Her short, curvy frame was swamped by it, and she looked so sexy. There is a thing us lads have; there isn't much sexier than a girl in your baggy shirts, even better when it's your team.

I sometimes wonder if you still have my old Saints away shirt. The blue one with "#1 Taz' on the back.

I walked up behind Alicia and slipped my arms around her. My lips touched her neck and I felt her body exhale with pleasure. Out of the corner of my eye I could see hers were closed, and a smile crept across her face.

'You still want to go on that walk?' I asked.

'Mm, do you think you could go again?'

'Maybe,' I said cheekily. Alicia's hands run up my arms and despite the sun shining I got goose bumps.

'Come on, we are only here for the night, I want to have a little explore,' she turned to face me and planted a kiss on my lips. My hands found her arse and I gave it a cheeky squeeze. 'No, off! Come on, let's go.'

'Okay, okay, let's go.'

We got dressed and then walked hand in hand out the back of the hotel. It loomed over us as we went towards the lake like a huge prop forward on the charge. The sun bounced off it and I was glad I had grabbed a pair of sunglasses on the way out. What's more I was glad I hadn't picked up my Gillet, I was already starting to sweat (the pre-walk workout might have constituted to that though).

'I'm glad we did this,' I said.

'Me too,' she replied.

I stopped abruptly and pulled her into me, gave her a kiss and said 'Alicia, I want to tell you something.'

'What?' she turned her head slightly, nervous. Not as nervous as I was, I'm sure. I was shitting my pants.

'I know we have only known each other a month or so.'

'Jamie, don't say what I think you're going to say. I'm not there yet.'

'No, me neither, but, if I'm honest, I'm falling, Alicia. I'm crazy about you.'

Alicia placed her hand behind my head and pulled me into her, kissing me.

'I'm crazy about you too,' she said. I smiled, a wave of relief flooding over my body. We continued to walk and our fingers were still interlocked. Alicia rested her head against my shoulder, her other hand wrapping around my arm and she kissed it. I kissed the top of her head.

I was so damn happy.

Jamie

***

St Helens, Merseyside, June 12th

Hours Slept:	6
Times we Had Sex:	5
Positions Attempted:	7
My Favourite Position:	Cowgirl
Mood:	Confused and angry

Dear Shona,

Something has happened. Something really bad. God, I'm still crying. I don't know who to turn to. Well I do, but you're not here, so I guess this letter will have to do. I don't know where to start. I'll just tell you about the day first.

We woke up at eight. The breakfast was delicious. Maybe I was just hungry from the late-night activities, maybe it was because it was a proper full English (eggs, bacon, sausage, hash browns, black pudding, mushrooms, beans in a separate pot and two slices of toast each) or maybe it was because I'd woken up in a posh hotel, with an incredible woman smiling at me and the sun shining in through a crack in the curtains. I was in such a good mood that a tripe and dog shit sandwich would have tasted good.

We ate up, started packing, had a quickie in the shower, finished packing and then left. Because Alicia had already paid online then it meant that the checkout was a breeze. We flung the bags into the back of the Capri and set off. We were in no rush so we decided to take a little detour. Alicia said she'd heard of this waterfall that was supposed to be cool called Aira Force, so after getting lost yet again, we found the National

Trust walk. I parked the car, paid the two-pound-whatever it was to park there and we set off.

Yeah, OK so I'm pretty thick when it comes to nature and all that, but even I had to admit it was gorgeous. It was about twenty-odd metres high and gushed over the rocks like a charging defensive line. There was a bridge going over it, so that as we walked over took a couple of pictures, which of course I put straight onto my Instagram. Alicia insisted on a romantic picture of us kissing with the waterfall in the background, so we found a clearing and she stretched out her arm to take the selfie.

It took us nigh on thirty efforts before she found one she liked. She either looked fat, or ugly, or I was pulling a stupid face, or the damn filter was playing up. Why do you girls take forever to take a photograph? Eventually, she got one she liked. If any of the lads saw it, they'd crucify me with banter, but deep down I thought it was quite a sweet picture. I just wasn't going to let Alicia think that. We slowly walked back to the car and I unlocked it, checking my phone.

There were two missed calls from Yozzer, and a text that read 'When are you back?' Damn, that reminded me I hadn't messaged Swifty back. Hurriedly I sent a message to Swifty saying 'It's been amazing pal, on our way back now' and then in response to Yozzer 'In about two hours, what's up?' Then I tossed the phone onto Alicia's lap and slid into the car.

'Hey, watch it,' she said.

'Look after it, will ya?' I replied, starting the engine.

'Yes, sir,' she said, giving me a sarcastic salute. I laughed, kissed her cheek and pulled out of the car park. The drive back down was just as nice as the one up. Alicia fell asleep and I kept looking over at her, her head resting against her hand.

She looked so peaceful, so beautiful. I smiled to myself and looked back at the road. Damn, it was good to be this happy again, it had been far too long.

It took us just over two hours to get back. I dropped Alicia off at hers, pulled her back in the car three times for an extra kiss and then drove the car home. I parked in my usual spot round the back, then wondered to the front door.

That's when I saw Yozzer waiting for me.

'Yoz, what's going on?' I said. Yozzer looked upset, it was almost as if he had been crying. What the hell was going on, had I done something?

'Let's go upstairs mate,' Yozzer said.

'OK, yeah sure come up...' I said, unlocking the door. We went to my flat where I dumped my duffel bag on my bed and Yozzer waited in the living room. I came back and said 'So what's going on.'

'Taz, it's Swifty,' Yozzer said, his voice wavering. A sudden sickness struck my stomach. I knew. I just fucking knew. Like I know that you know what I'm about to tell you.

'What about him?' I asked anyway.

'He's... Mate he's...' Yozzer struggled to get the words out.

'Jesus Christ mate, what is it.'

'He's killed himself. Last night, his flatmate found him this morning hanging from his curtain rail.'

I've been hit by twenty-stone prop forwards. I've been drilled to the floor by some absolute beasts. I've had my arse handed to me in fights. But this hit me like a eighteen-wheeler. My entire body went numb. My brain shut off. My mouth went dry. I needed you. I needed Alicia. I needed someone, anyone.

'Is this some kind of joke?' was all I could muster. I looked at Yozzer. He had been crying, because a tear was forming in his eye again and his jaw started shaking as he shook his head.

'There was a note, Taz,' Yozzer said, 'down at the police station. The coppers, have said we can read it when we are ready, as we are both named in it.'

'Swifty's dead?' was all I said.

'Yeah man, he's dead.'

That's when it happened. The dam burst. Aira Force had absolutely nothing on me. I fell into Yozzer's arms and he held me tight, tighter than anyone had ever held me before.

'I should have known,' I blubbered, 'I should have done something.'

'None of us knew, mate,' Yozzer said, and I could tell he was holding back his own tears, 'he didn't tell anyone.'

'He messaged last night asking how my weekend was. I should have replied, I could have talked to him, you know?'

'Don't, don't even start that,' Yozzer suddenly became stern and let me go, holding me at arm's length.

'We could have spoken and I could have helped him.'

'Do not start the blame game, mate. This isn't anyone's fault. No one knew!'

'We should have seen it!' I shouted.

'Seen what? Mate he was always happy around us! How were we supposed to know?'

'Because we're his best mates! We should have been there! Why didn't he tell us?'

'You saw him last weekend. He was happy, smiling. How the hell were we supposed to know about it?'

I fell back onto the sofa and held my head in my hands. Above me, the police called Yozzer about the support on offer and some other shit but I couldn't concentrate. I couldn't believe it. I just couldn't believe it. All I could think of was imagining my best mate's body swinging from the neck. Sick, I know. I know you barely knew him, but I had to tell you. Or write it down or what-fucking-ever I don't know. Jesus Christ Shona I need you more than anything right now. Why aren't you here?

Jamie.

***

St Helens, June 13th

Hours Slept:	Barely Any
Hours Worked:	Zero
Anti-Depressants:	Two More Than Normal
Suicidal Thoughts:	Three

Dear Shona,

The ceiling was still cream.

I'd been staring at it for the past few hours. It was now midday on Monday and nothing had happened. My eyes stung from tiredness and tears. My boss had heard the news the night before; he was friends with Swifty's folks. He messaged me and told me not to come in on Monday.

So I didn't.

All I wanted was for you to be here and be in your arms. No one else's. Yours.

I was told there was a note that Swifty had left. Yozzer had said we had been mentioned. I didn't want to read it. Not just yet. About a million thoughts had been running through my head, reading that would just add to it. Alicia had messaged last night and this morning when she had woken up. I had yet to reply to the second message. I hadn't even opened the message. I wasn't concerned, she would be worried, more than likely, but she thought I was a hell of a lot stronger than I was. She didn't know about the darkness.

I moved so that I was lying on my side, my duvet wrapped around me, cocooning me from everything. My curtains were still drawn. Through a slight crack I could see that today the sun was shining and it was a bright, sunny June day. Not in my room it wasn't. Not in my head.

I was so tired. I could barely keep my eyes open and yet they remained that way. My body was drained, more so than after a full eighty. It didn't want to respond to anything, not that I wanted it to move anyway. Instead, I lay there, staring at nothing. Eventually, after letting a few more tears roll down my face, I responded to Alicia's text, just letting her know I was fine. I hated lying to her. But what could I do? Then, I went back to the ceiling.

Jamie.

***

St Helens, June 14th

Hours Slept:	Who Cares?
Food eaten:	God Knows
Texts sent:	None
Antidepressants:	None
Suicidal Thoughts:	Twelve

Dear Shona,
   Update; the ceiling is still cream.

Jamie.

***

St Helens, June 15ᵗʰ

Hours Slept:	A Couple
Food Eaten:	Half a Frozen Pizza
Texts Sent:	Two
Antidepressants:	One
Suicidal Thoughts:	Three

Dear Shona,

I went back to work on Wednesday, but I barely worked. My head just wasn't in it. You can only imagine what it's like. My supervisor, Jim, the same guy who said don't bother with Monday, was decent with me. He made sure I didn't use the forklift, which was probably a good idea. I just did some of the paperwork instead. You know, sort out orders and shit like that. The morning dragged and I was so tired. My body felt beat. My brain was on auto pilot. It's amazing what it can do. You know when you do such menial tasks, without thinking, and they just get done? My mind was wondering. I thought about Swifty and how I wish I'd just responded to that damn message on Saturday night. It wouldn't have taken much. Just a simple 'it's good mate, how are you?' and it would all have been fine. Do you think I had been a bad friend?

Then I thought about all the times I'd cancelled, most recently a couple for Alicia. I never used to do that. In fact, you would tell me not to cancel on the boys for you. I can imagine you shaking your head at me. I'm just paranoid Alicia will change her mind on me. Like you did.

Swifty just needed someone, I know that's what it is like for me. I could have been there for him. I could have told him what was going on with myself. The coppers had said his medical record said he wasn't on any drugs for anything. I could have spoken to him and given him advice. He could have been on the head pills, like me. We could have talked about what was bringing us down, whatever it was for him. I knew then that I had to read the note, find out why he was depressed. If it was similar as mine I could have helped. Even if it wasn't I could have helped.

I should have helped.

It's my fault he's dead, isn't it? Be honest.

I started crying over a sofa order form.

It came out of nowhere. The boss sent me home, probably for the best. At home I continued to cry for an hour or so. After a while it wasn't even over Swifty or my own guilt. After a while I was just crying because that's what I did, until I ran out of tears. What would you say if you could see me now? What would you think of me?

The Monster was back, Shona.

Had the bastard even left? Who knows, who cares. If it never left it had hidden itself well in the deep, dark recesses of my mind, right at the back where I couldn't see it. Now it was clawing at me, reasserting its grip on me, squeezing me tighter and tighter until the last remnants of happiness had been oozed out of me. Damn, I'd been so happy, with rugby, the boys, Alicia. I had even stopped writing the letters to you. I guess when I feel like shit, I need you.

I hadn't thought about Alicia all day. Neither had you for a bit. Swifty had been on my mind, of course he had. I'd messaged her generic 'I'm OK' messages, but we'd barely talked.

I wonder if she was worried about me. Would you be? Why the hell would she be worried about me? Why would anyone be worried about me? I can barely keep my life in check. She'll leave me when it all comes to much, like everyone else, like you did, like Swifty.

The wave came back over. My tear ducts must have replenished. How could I blame Swifty like that? I knew exactly what he was going through. I can't blame him for what he's done to us. People will call him selfish, because of the impact it will have, but damn people like that. It was his decision, his life. He was miserable, clearly. So miserable he couldn't take it anymore. How dare people call him selfish.

My phone pinged with a message.

I dried my eyes, sniffed loudly and picked up the phone; a WhatsApp from Alicia.

'Hey, are you All right today? Haven't heard from you and getting worried xxx.'

'I got sent home from work, I miss him xxx.'

'Oh babe, I know you miss him. I'll come over after work xxx.'

It wasn't a question, or a request, it was a decisive 'I'll come over', and that's what I needed. I contemplated saying no, but that would cause and argument and she was damn stubborn, so instead I sent back 'OK xxx'. Before I tossed my phone aside I saw it was nearly five o'clock anyway. I could have another hour blissfully torturous alone time first. The truth is, I wanted it to be you coming over.

I spent that hour staring back at my favourite ceiling (it's still cream, in case you're wondering). We were becoming good friends. I knew everything about it, all the cracks and best line for a spider to take. It didn't judge me.

Alicia arrived not long after six. She held me for at least ten minutes. Neither of us said anything, she just held me. My hand gripped her hair tightly, my other pulled her in close. For a few minutes, I pretended she was you even though I hadn't seen her since hearing about Swifty. We went through to my room and sat on the bed.

'Have you been taking your pills?' she asked me.

I shook my head.

'Jamie, you have to take them, I'm getting worried about you.'

'Are you?'

'Yes! Fucking hell, Jamie, of course I care about you!'

'I hope you do.'

'Don't Jamie. Don't start this.'

'Start what?'

'Questioning. Pushing me away. You mean the world to me. Have you been eating?'

I nodded.

'And have you been eating proper foods?'

I shook my head. No point lying now, there were takeaway boxes strewn over the floor.

'OK, I'm gonna make you dinner tonight, I'll take you to mine and you can stay with me, get you out of here.'

'You don't like it when I stay in the week. You can't sleep proper.'

'Not quite as important as you, Jamie, is it? Where are your pills?'

'I'll pack my stuff.'

'Will you heckers like, I'll make sure you have everything. Now where are they?'

I pointed at the drawer of my bedside table. Alicia stood up and went to it, pulled it open and started to move things around looking for the pills. I put my head in my hands and started to rub my face and my temples.

'Jamie, what the hell is this?'

I looked up at her. She had opened an old pencil case I kept my test in and pulled out a fresh needle, still in its packet. I didn't say anything. Alicia pulled out the vial of testosterone.

'Jamie, what the fuck? What is this?'

Again, I said nothing. She moved the pencil case and pulled out the plastic spoon I got the first time I exchanged a needle. They'd stopped giving me them after that.

'Are you shooting up?'

'No, no it's not like that,' I said, barely raising my voice. I was too tired to fight.

'Then you'd better tell me right now what's going on! If you're taking drugs Jamie, we have a massive problem!'

'It's not a drug, it's a hormone.'

'What? What are you talking about?'

'It's testosterone.'

'Steroids. You're taking steroids.'

'No, well kind of, these aren't illegal.'

'Are you kidding me right now?'

'Seriously, I can't get in trouble for this...'

'You think that's what I care about?! You getting into trouble? Jesus Christ Jamie, I know this is hard for you but you gotta start looking after yourself! And now steroids? Are you serious right now?'

'It's not a steroid!' I shouted. Looks like the fight was on.

'Don't start playing semantics, Jamie, of course it's a

fucking steroid!'

'It's a hormone, it's perfectly safe, I'm taking it safely, I don't see what the big deal is here?'

'The big deal is you aren't taking your medication but you're happy to stick a needle in your arm and inject yourself with God knows what!'

'It doesn't go in my arm, and I know what it is!'

'Where did you get it from?'

'What?'

'Where did you get it from?'

'What does it matter where I got it from?'

'Jesus Jamie, just tell me where you got it from!'

'A guy, a guy at the gym.'

'Then how do you know what it is?'

'Because there's a batch number and the seal wasn't broken! Fuck's sake Alicia, stop acting like I'm stupid!'

'You are fucking stupid putting this shit in your body!'

The air suddenly became cold. A familiar feeling of rage and hurt coursed through me. The rage went quickly, but the stabbing pain of Alicia's thoughts towards me remained.

'Get out,' I said.

'Jamie…'

'I said get out. Leave my stuff and get out.'

Alicia didn't move. She still held the needle and vial and her breathing was deep. She looked over at me and I avoided her eye contact. Putting the needle and vial down on the bedside table she approached me.

'I'm not leaving, Jamie.'

'Please, Alicia, please just get out.'

'No. I'm not leaving you like this.'

'GET OUT!' That was the first time I ever yelled at her, and it didn't stop, 'GET OUT, GET OUT!' I fell to the bed and started to cry again. Alicia sat down next to me.

'It's OK, Jamie, It's OK, I'm here.'

'I'm sorry,' I stammered through tears.

'Shh, it's fine. Just calm down. I'm sorry I got angry.'

I cried for a further fifteen minutes whilst Alicia held me, occasionally playing with my hair and kissing my head. When I was ready, I got up, packed an overnight bag, grabbed my pills and followed Alicia to hers. She made me a curry she'd had sent in from one of those weekly mail order meal things and it was pretty nice; she wasn't a bad chef. We didn't speak much that evening, which was fine with me. Instead, we curled up in bed and I fell asleep in her arms.

And after all she did, all of that, I still kind of wished it was you. Where are you, Shona, where are you? What are you doing and who are you doing it with? I need you now more than anything. You know me better than anyone. The longing, the pain, it's too much. Please Shona. Please come home soon.

Jamie.

***

Sutton Phoenix v Orrell St James, June 18ᵗʰ

Starting Position:	Full Back
Mood:	Low
Pre-game Fat Burners:	4
Warm Up:	Solid
Antidepressants:	Still citalopram

Dear Shona,

I'm sorry about that last letter. These emotions are getting the better of me. Swifty's dead, I still miss you. I'm depressed, again. Life is tough. But we still had a season to play, and I couldn't let the boys down. Next we played Orrell St James.

We held a minute's silence before the game. Fair play to them, they had offered to postpone the game until a later date, but we knew that isn't what Swifty would have wanted. So we played the game. It was an odd atmosphere in the changing rooms before the game. Usually there were players bouncing around, getting into the zone. Swifty would always sit below his peg, a pair of headphones in, as he listened to some drum n bass and focus himself. It was odd to see the young sixteen-year-old we had called up from the juniors. I think he was a centre, but at our level he would be fine on the wing.

He was no Swifty though.

We would usually play Gimme Shelter by *The Rolling Stones* before we walked out onto the pitch, kind of a Phoenix tradition. Today, we didn't play anything. We huddled as usual in the middle of the room, our arms around one another, grabbing onto the player besides shirt. I had Yozzer on my left, Samoa on my right.

'All right lads, I don't need to say much today,' Skip said, 'this one is for Swifty. Everything you do today, you think of that lad who used to give his all for you. Every run, every metre you make, every try you score, that is for him today.'

God I wanted to score today. More than anything I wanted a try today. I was more of your creative full back, an extra half back, but today I knew I wanted to score. There was a strange willingness in my stomach to get over that try line and dot one down. I had to score today. I just had to. Skip finished off his team talk.

'So do your jobs, don't do anything different and we'll beat these boys and get Swifty the W, get upstairs and have a drink for him. Squeeze on three, one, two, three!'

The entire circle of players pushed towards the centre, our shoulders crushing into one another and we cried out 'SQUEEZE!' and we made our way to the pitch. Another thing you never understood. Didn't you once tell me it was idiotic? I think you did.

The minute's silence was impeccable. Remember that one we did for Mac's dad? Where we stand on the halfway, both teams looking at the clubhouse? Maybe you weren't there.

The game started a little cagey. I guess no one wanted to make any mistakes. Not today. They kicked off and I got underneath it, playing in towards the clubhouse, and I caught the ball, offloading it to Mac who took the first carry. Three Orrell players hit him hard and he played the ball on the twenty. Our first exit set went well. I'll give the young lad his dues (he had been given the nickname 'Kid', another imaginative name from Mac) he was enthusiastic and had a decent step on him. He took a little scoot from Mac's play the ball and made an extra ten metres or so. Carl took the next carry and then Samoa. Yozzer decided to kick on the fourth, something he liked to do a lot, trying to catch them short at the back. It wasn't the best kick though and their full back ran it back towards centre field.

They didn't offer much going forward and we got a turnover on our own ten. Carl started our set off and Skip made a half break. We got a second tackle at around halfway and Skip's quick play the ball lead to the first try. Jimmy scooted as the defence tried to get back onside but they weren't quick enough. Yozzer and I were steaming rolling in support and Jimmy hit Yozzer with a tip pass. He broke the defenceive line with ease and I ran alongside him. Their full back with pretty small and chunky, looked more like a second rower or a hooker, and Yozzer drew him in. Just before contact he passed across to me and I had a straight run under the sticks. I dove across the line and touched the ball down.

Standing, I yelled louder than I had ever yelled, right from the bottom of my lungs. I threw the ball in the air and clenched my fists and dropped to my knees, raising my arms and pointing at the sky.

That were for Swifty.

The rest of the team descended on me, drowning me in a sea of orange and yellow. That try meant so much to everyone. The clubhouse was cheering louder than when we beat Thatto last year with the last play of the game. It had to be, didn't it? Yozzer to me for the first try. I could barely breath at the bottom of the pile on but it was worth it. Somewhere, on the other side of the bodies, I could hear the ref, 'All right lads, come on, let's get the conversion taken.'

'Sorry sir,' one of the players, I don't know who, said, and the players on top of me started to move off.

'It's OK,' the ref said. 'Time's off.'

I shook a fist in celebration at our supporters to a chorus of cheers, 'Get in there Taz,' and 'Ata boy, Taz!' I ran back to reposition myself for the restart. Wish you'd seen me score that. I know Swifty did.

We got two more tries before half time, Carl in the corner and Mac crashing over from close range. Yozzer converted all of them and we led 18-4 at half time. We had leaked a try on the edge but to be fair to Orrell it were a damn good try and nothing we could have done to stop it.

In the middle of the field we supped down water and took a minute to catch our breath. Skip patted me on the back and then addressed the team.

'Good half lads, but it aint over yet. We know what these boys are like, they are gonna keep coming and keep coming. Nowt we could do about that try, but we should have snuffed it earlier. They attack well from the left channel, so if we can hold them central or right, we've got 'em all day long,' he said. We all nodded. 'Hey, lads grab a shirt,' Skip continued and we created another circle. 'Let's not forget why we are playing today. Swifty on three, one, two three...'

'SWIFTY!'

A bit different to the squeeze, but probably too American for you. For once though, Shona, I don't think I would care if you liked it or not. Today was about Swifty.

They pulled two more back early in the second half. First, another sweeping move to the edge caught us out and then some sloppy tackling meant their loose forward was able to dance his way over. They converted both of them to make it 18-16. Skip gave us a right rollicking after their latest kick went over.

'What did I say? They would keep coming, we've switched off! Fucking hell boys, I am not, I repeat I AM NOT prepared to lose this game! Not today!' he yelled at us. I nodded along with him. That last try was a little my fault. OK, so the big boys in the front line should have wrapped him up, but their loose forward wasn't anything special, just bulky. When he had broken through, he tried to step me and I attempted to tackle him around his chest. Massive mistake. I should have taken his legs. I would have brought him down and had them on their last tackle ten out. But because I went high, he brushed me aside easily. I could feel my head drop as we jogged back to take our kick-off when Skip's voice was suddenly in my ear.

'Head up Taz, it's one missed tackle. He's watching mate, he dunt want that head to drop.'

We got a break. A slightly shorter kick-off from Yozzer caught Orrell napping and it bounced awkwardly, causing their wiry half back to knock it on. With that set we got into position and Yozzer dabbed an awkward little grubber through for Samoa to grab a try after it ricocheted off the posts. Yozzer slotted the conversion and we had a little breathing space. He'd brought his kicking boots, that was for sure.

We exchanged set after set, neither team willing to budge defensively. It was going to come down to a mistake, either one from us to let Orrell back into it, or from them to let us put a three-score buffer between us. But the mistake came from me. Yozzer played a ball out the back to me and I took my eyes off the ball. We were on our own forty and the ball bobbled on my fingertips. As it hit the ground I lashed out at it in frustration and the ref blew up. I could imagine you shaking your head from the touchline, disappointed at my reaction. You know I don't lash out. But before I go into details, it gets worse. You wouldn't be proud. Not even sure why I want to tell you. Suppose I want you to see how I'm feeling.

'OK, knock on here, no advantage, scrum down, St James head and feed,' he said. I wrapped the side of my head with the heal of my hand as a couple of my team mates, I'm not sure who, patted my shoulders and ruffled my hair. I took my place at the back of the scrum as the ball was played out by their hooker and I retreated to my full back position. They took three up front carries and on the fourth tackle they were in that left thirty channel. We knew what was coming so I watched as the defence set themselves. I scanned across, making sure there were no kinks the chain. It all looked good to me.

Two plays out the back with their full back sweeping around to take it at third. He gave a double pump to the centre which released the number three into a hole. I had swept across to cover the back, but now I had a two on one, where I was the one. I had a choice, either go for the ball and hope he doesn't pass or anticipate the pass and take out the winger, hoping he didn't dummy. I hated these choices. What would you have had me done? I was suddenly imagining you watching again.

As they approached, I locked eyes on the ball. I had to tackle the ball carrier. But then they pulled something new out of their sleeve. The winger ran around the back of the centre in a drop off and I was left flat footed as the centre popped the pass. I tried to turn quickly but my foot slipped. There was a gap between me and our winger as well. I was on our own ten metre line, so I had to be quick. I chased the winger back and attempted the tackle. As we went down over the line I shifted my body weight, trying to roll under the winger, but it was in vein. He got the ball down. The ref jogged behind us, pointed at the spot the ball had been grounded and gave a long blast of his whistle. The winger and I stood up. Ball in hand he celebrated in my face, his arms outstretched, a cocky grin on his face.

'Come on!' he yelled. I snapped. With two hands I pushed the cocky prick backwards and grabbed him around the scruff of his neck. Players came streaming in from both teams, pulling us apart. The winger still had his cocky smile. I wanted to wipe it off his face with a right hook. I know, I know, it wasn't like me. You know I'm no fighter. But can you blame me? On today of all days?

'Taz, Taz, calm down pal!' Skip was screaming at me. Yozzer had rushed in and slipped his arm between the winger and me.

'Not today mate,' he said into my ear. My stare hadn't left the arrogant bastard's smile, but when Yozzer spoke I looked at him. His face was stern, his eyes piercing me. The ref was blowing his whistle, like it was some kind of riot siren, and I released the winger.

'Number one, number five, come here now!' the ref yelled. I went over to him with Skip and their winger went with their captain, 'right, I know this game has a little extra to it but it's been good so far, don't drop it now. Five, celebrate like that again and it's ten minutes in the bin, you understand?' the winger nodded. 'And number one, react like that again and it's ten minutes, OK?' I nodded. 'Good, go back to your teams.'

'Come on Taz, keep your head mate, can't afford to drop

to twelve against these boys,' Skip said to me as we walked to our huddle. Their little wiry half back kicked the conversion and it was suddenly a two-point game again. After the restart Orrell exited well, but after they kicked deep, which I collected and gave to the Kid to return, we won a penalty; markers not square. Yozzer belted downfield and we had an attacking set on their forty. First two carries from us were good, our forwards making good yards towards the middle of the field. Then we jacked the play and attacked the left. I shifted over, an extra pass from where I usually started on these plays. It went to Samoa, who gave me the ball. I looked up. Perfect, the two players in front of me were the centre and the cocky winger. I lined up the winger and ran at him.

OK, I'm not proud of this Shona, but I'll tell you what I did. I raised my forearms with the ball protected underneath and caught the prick just right; square on his jaw. He tried to tackle me and we both fell. As I got to my feet, I was the one being grabbed around the scruff of my neck. It was their centre.

'What are you doing?' he spat through his gumshield. Players rushed in, again trying to separate us. Skip wrenched me away. The winger was groggily getting to his feet.

'What did I just say?' he growled, a tight wad of my shirt in his fist. Again, the referee was blowing his whistle as a fight threatened to break out.

'Come here!' he snapped at me and Skip, 'I didn't see what happened, so I can't do anything. I saw two players go down and the number four has gone in on you. This is a team warning. Same goes for Orrell St James, team warning. Next time, I don't care who it is, someone goes in the bin, understand?'

'Yes sir,' some of the players chorused. Coach had appeared

on the touchline by where the tackle had taken place.

'Taz! Taz! Get here! Come off for ten, cool off a bit!'

I hung my head and jogged off the pitch as one of the inter-changes, a smaller but athletic guy called Darrell, ran on to my place, strapping up a black head guard. I snatched a water bottle and sank down on the bench. Coach patted me on the shoulder. I know you're not impressed, but that's not why I'm telling you.

I didn't get back on that game. It was fine though, Carl got another to add to his tally after a smart cross field kick from Yozzer and then no one scored after that. In the showers, I barely spoke. I just washed myself, got dressed and looked to leave. I walked out to the car park, unlocked my car and threw my bag in the back. You want to know what I was thinking about? This sounds crude, Shona, but I needed to fuck you. I had so much aggression pent up from that prick on the wing, I needed to let it out. Alicia wasn't like you. She didn't like being thrown around or choked. But that's what I needed right now. And I know you would love it. Remember the times I was pissed off and we went half the night? Or that game last season when the ref was shit, I was so pissed off I came home, we barely spoke a word and I basically ripped your clothes off. That was the best sex we ever had. Well today I was raging, think about how good it would have been. Imagine that.

'Oi, Taz, where you going?' I looked over my shoulder to see Yozzer walking over to me.

'Home. I'm going home.'

'Why you going home?'

'Cause I'm tired.'

'We need to pour one out for Swifty.'

'I just want to go home mate.'

'First game after your best mate dies and you won't even have a beer for him?' Yozzer shook his head and turned around. Sly. Very sly. But he was right.

'Don't.' I said shortly.

'Don't what?'

'Play that shit with me.'

'Taz mate, we all feel shitty. We just got a good win and no one cares because we all feel shitty. And this is Swifty. Swifty loved playing Orrell. I know things got heated but you got a try and now you can have a beer and we can remember that sappy bastard for what he was. Our best mate.'

Yozzer didn't half talk sense sometimes. He was the biggest lad out of all of us, yet he had a level head. I laughed. Sappy bastard. Yeah, Swifty was one. He was probably looking down saying 'Shut up Yozzer!'. I welled up a little as I heard his voice in my head.

'All right,' I said, 'come on, lead the way.'

I locked my car and Yozzer put his arm around me. We walked back into the clubhouse and up to the bar. Skip rang the bell.

'OK, man of the matches, for Orrell, your loose forward!' the big number thirteen who had crashed over walked up to get his port and pint.

'And for Sutton,' their halfback and captain began, 'your number seven,' unsurprisingly, Yozzer got man of the match. He had been outstanding. Swifty would have been so proud of him.

'And a debut, but he's only sixteen so the lucky bastard gets away with it!' the club house cheer for the Kid. His mum were with him, so even though usually we'd sneak him some drink, this time Skip thought better of it, 'and today, there's no Dickhead of the Day. Instead, I just want to say a few words. Thanks, Orrell for coming and putting this game on. We've spoken and decided that now every year this fixture will be the Danny Swift Memorial Game, and we'll have a trophy done,' a massive cheer went up, the loudest coming from Yozzer and I. We had made our way to the front and were clapping so hard. Yozzer put an arm around me and squeezed my shoulder. I gave Skip the thumbs up, 'Swifty was a massive part of this club and was the top try scorer for the past two years. He scored some unforgettable tries and some important tries. He was loved by everyone involved with the club and will be sorely, sorely missed. So I'd like to raise a glass to our good friend and teammate, Dan Swift.'

I felt a tear run down my cheek as I raised my pint glass as everyone inside the clubhouse said in unison 'to Swifty!'. Yozzer turned to face me as the men of the match did their port and beer.

'I didn't want you to miss that, mate.'

'I know. Cheers pal,' I nodded.

'I miss him.'

'Me too.'

'Let's have a couple here, then if you want we can go for one in town, or go back and play some FIFA at mine and chill.'

'Swifty were always the best at FIFA.'

'Let's do that then,' Yozzer smiled. We clinked our glasses together and joined the rest of the team.

I'm at home now. Yozzer beat me at FIFA, but I wanted to get this letter down. I've been writing them in this book I got, so even though I probably could have written this at Yozzer's, I wanted to write it in the same book. Decided if I do send them, I'll send them all together. It's only a cheap thing from Wilkos, but I've decided after everything that has happened I didn't want to end up ripping them. I really wish you'd seen that game today. Maybe my head would have been more level and I wouldn't have lost it at that poor winger. He wasn't that bad, I suppose, just the wrong day. Could have done with you there. Oh well, maybe one day.

Jamie.

***

St Helens Police Station, June 20th

Hours Slept:	Four to Five
Food Eaten:	Nothing
Anti-Depressants:	left at home
Suicidal Thoughts:	Four

Dear Shona,

Today was the day. The day Yozzer and I had agreed to go and read Swifty's suicide note. I took a picture on my phone so I can recite it perfectly to you. I want you to see what he wrote about me.

Work had given me the day off again; my boss was being pretty understanding about the whole thing. Same with Yozzer's, apparently. So I stayed at his on Sunday night and we had a little lie in. Though I don't suppose lying on my side and staring at the wall and biting my nails can really be classed a lie in. Then, at 10am we got up, dressed and headed over to the cop shop.

Neither of us spoke in the car on the way over. I had never really seen Yozzer like this before, he'd never been this quiet. I guess he was thinking about the letter as well. The coppers had said both him and I were mentioned. All I could think about was what that could possibly be. Was Swifty blaming us? Was he saying we should have been better friends? Was it an apology? The paranoia of it all was incredible. Could have done with you holding my hand, but to be honest it was probably best just Yozzer and I went.

I was surprised I was able to drive. But before I knew it we were there. How, I have no idea, I had been barely able to concentrate on the road. I must have been on autopilot.

A stern-looking policewoman checked us in, and though she seemed hard, she softened when she found out the nature of our visit. We took a seat and sat again in silence. I was nervous, and so was Yozzer, I could tell. He had pursed his lips to exhale and the only time I had seen him sit and breathe like that was in the semi-final of the cup last year. Could have done with holding your hand. A uniformed officer came out to meet us.

'Hi lads, I'm PC Brown, do you want to come with me?' he motioned us into the station. We followed him into one of the interrogation rooms, you know what they look like. 'Here you are, we thought you'd like some privacy to read this. I'll be outside if any of it becomes too much for you, do either of you want a tea or coffee?'

'I'll have a brew, two sugars, thanks,' Yozzer said, though the words were jovial, he wasn't. There was a sadness in his voice, it wasn't as bouncy as usual. I shook my head.

'All right, I'll come back with that then leave you to read the note in private,' PC Brown left the room and we sat down on the same side of the table, our backs to the door. Yozzer turned to me.

'You all right pal?' he asked. I shrugged.

'As well I will be.'

'Listen, we'll read this, then why don't we go have lunch at the pub?'

'OK.'

'And we can talk about it, or not, or whatever.'

'All right, yeah man,' I was looking at my hands, which were picking at the cuticles of my fingers. Behind us, the door opened.

'Here's your tea, and here's the note. If you could keep it in the plastic wallet we'd appreciate that. Take your time, and I'll be waiting outside,' and with that, he left. Yozzer and I looked at each other and took a deep breath. The note sat in between us, and I recognised Swifty's handwriting straight away.

'OK, let's do this,' Yozzer said, his arm finding its way around me and squeezing me shoulder in support. I nodded and started to read. Here is what he wrote.

To whoever finds this,

Honestly, don't know what to write. I've thought time and time again what I'd put on this when I finally got the courage to do what I'm about to do, but now I've got the pen in my hand I don't know what to put.

Mum, Dad, I'm sorry. I'm sorry for everything. I'm sorry I couldn't amount to what you guys thought I could. This is not your fault, you always supported me, through uni, through all the shit jobs, everything. But that's just it. It's just shit jobs. I got the lowest grade at uni, so no wonder no one wants to hire someone like me. I've let you down. I could have been so much more but I guess that's not the type of person I am. I always be at the bottom of the pile. I wish I could have been better. I wish I could have made you proud but the truth is I'm just not good enough to do that. I'm not that person, who can push myself. I guess I'm scared, scared of more failure.

Taz and Yozzer, my best friends. I wish I had had the guts to tell you how I was feeling. I don't think you would understand how it feels to be this low, feel like an outcast, the one who can't get the girls, the one right at the back, the one no one notices, the quiet one, the scared one. I was scared of what you would think of me. Because the truth is I've been thinking about doing this for a long time now.

I'm tired, so tired of being rejected. Every woman I meet, they reject me. I'm not good enough for anyone. I've heard that saying, it's better to have loved and lost than never to have loved at all. It must be true, I have no idea what love is, if I've ever felt it. Certainly, no one has ever felt it for me. A kiss on the cheek and 'you're my best friend'. Then they never talk to me again. Rejection after rejection. Put that with losing the Leigh contract, it just adds up. I'm tired of not being good enough, or something coming along to ruin everything. I could have been a pro, I could have played for England, and actually been somebody. But I'm not. I'm a nobody.

It's all just too much for me now. I'm tired of it all and I want it to stop. I want the pain to stop. Inside, every morning, every night, I wake up and go to sleep with pain and a loneliness, crying myself to sleep. I can't take it anymore and I want it all to stop. This is the only way that it will. I don't want this life anymore. I don't want to live anymore.

I'm sorry for everything.

Daniel.

I finished a few seconds before Yozzer did. I raised my hand and started to bite the skin next to my nail, staring at the wall opposite. Allow me it just this once. I can imagine you wincing as I write this, but come on. Yozzer placed both his hands on the table and breathed deeply.

'Wow,' he said, 'that were tough.'

'Yeah.'

'You All right?'

'Yeah.'

We sat in silence for a couple of minutes. I just stared at the wall and continued to bite at my fingers. Eventually, Yozzer put his hand on my shoulder again.

'Come on, let's go Spoons or something. We'll have a pub lunch and we can talk about Swifty, if you want?'

'I'd like that.'

We stood up and left the letter on the table. Outside the interrogation room PC Brown approached us.

'All done?'

'Yes, thank you,' Yozzer said.

'Listen, this is a number of a local support group, if you need someone to talk to,' the officer handed us a business card with a telephone number on it. Yozzer took it, as I was barely paying attention, 'there are people out there who can help you if you need it.'

We thanked him and left. Again, we drove in complete silence. I parked my car in the usual back street and we walked over to St Helens' Wetherspoons, The Glass House. I wasn't very hungry, so got a ham egg and chips, you know, my usual, and Yozzer ordered a bacon and cheeseburger. We both got a pint of lager in. Then we found a table in a booth and slid in. I pulled my phone out of my pocket and checked for the first time since we had arrived at the police station. I had a text from Alicia.

'How was it? Are you OK? Xxx.'

'Alicia?' Yozzer asked me and I nodded, 'how has she been?'

'She's been great, had a barny last week, but she's been supportive.'

'What were the barny about?'

'Doesn't matter,' I said starting to type the response. 'It's sorted now. Just a little tiff.'

'So long as you're all good,' Yozzer raised the pint glass to his lips and I typed the rest of the message.

'Tough, but I'm OK, with Yozzer still. When can I see you this week? Xxx.' I placed the phone down on the table when I was done.

'Swifty absolutely hated Spoons,' Yozzer said. I snorted.

'Yeah, he really did.'

'He always said, there's more atmosphere at a funeral.'

'There will be at his.'

'Doesn't he have Irish family?'

'Yeah, on his mum's side.'

'Bloody hell, you ever been to an Irish wake?'

'Nope.

'It'll be a proper good send off for him, whenever it is.'

I nodded my head, 'We'll make sure it is.'

The food arrived quite quickly, not surprisingly as they probably just shoved it in the fryer and microwave, nice and easy.

'He always liked The Sefton, didn't he?' Yozzer asked, smothering his chips in tomato sauce.

'Oh aye, he loved it there.'

'And Punch Tarmey.'

'We all love it there.'

'And he hated Kazbar!'

Again, I snorted, 'It just weren't his scene.'

'He never were one for clubs or loud bars, were he?'

'Yet we always dragged him there.'

There was a moment of silence, and I wondered if the same sensation of guilt went through Yozzer. Do you think he resented us dragging him there? I put my knife and fork down as my phone buzzed. Alicia had replied.

'Glad you're OK babe, I'm not free until Friday night if you want to do something after work? Xxx.'

A stabbing pain hit me in the chest, like that of rejection. That's what it felt like, anyway, rejection. Was that feeling silly? You'd have made time for me, if we still were speaking, right?

'Oh, OK then, yeah I could come over after work xxx,' I typed back.

'Are you all right?' Yozzer asked, looking at me with his forehead wrinkled. The bastard was a mind reader, I swear.

'Yeah, fine, Alicia, just can't see her till Friday.'

'That's not so bad,' Yozzer shoved the burger back into his mouth.

'I suppose, just wonder why she's so busy, she knows I need her.'

'Don't start, Taz.'

'Don't start what?'

'Being Taz.'

'What are you talking about it?'

'You do this whenever you really like someone. Get paranoid. She has a tough job, right? It's probably that. You aint known her that long, mate.'

'I suppose so,' I shrugged.

'Trust me, mate. I've seen you do this before. Remember Liv, that bird before Shona? You scared her off, you were too much.'

'Yes, I get I scared her off. But my best mate hadn't just died.

And last week Alicia said… well I said it as well… she said she were falling for me.'

'Just be careful mate,' Yozzer put his burger down, this was getting serious, 'I don't want you getting hurt. I can tell you like this bird, and I know you probably need her sometimes. I know it's more difficult for you. Just, be careful, OK?'

He's right, isn't he? I was reasonably well behaved with you. At least I thought I was. I tried to give you your space. Sometimes though, I remember, you said I was too much. I remember you didn't say 'I love you' when I did. I said it far too early, yes I know. But sometimes you just feel it. I'll never forget when you did say it to me though. We were lying in bed, listening to music having a laugh. Things went quiet for a second and you just said it to me. I remember how good it felt to hear you say those words. I miss it.

'OK. Thanks pal. I really appreciate that,' I said to Yozzer.

'You're me best mate,' Yozzer picked his burger back up, pulling a lettuce leaf out of it.

'You too, I love ya mate.'

'Don't be a bender!'

'You know what I mean!'

'I'm joking. I love ya too, you bell end.'

I laughed. I did love the bastard, even when he was like this. I don't think I would have been able to read that letter with any of the other lads. I ate up the rest of my food and then we agreed to go somewhere else. The Wheatsheaf wasn't too far, so we headed there. A couple of pints of smooth later and we were on the fruity, slipping pound coins into the slot and yo-yoing between being ten pounds up and having to shove a fiver in. I pulled my phone out to see a message from Alicia had come in.

'OK, yeah come to mine Friday night, I'll make us a spaghetti carbonara, I just got a decent recipe! Xxx.'

'Wish I could see you tonight xxx,' I wrote back. Probably a mistake, but I did want to see her. I wandered what her plans were, why was she so busy before Friday? You're a woman, was she pushing me away?

'Damnit!' Yozzer said, hitting the machine, 'you got another fiver?'

'How much have we put in this already?'

'It's gonna pay out. Swifty would always give me an extra fiver…'

'Oh don't play that card!'

'Come on, one more.'

'Fine,' I said, pulling my wallet it out and handing Yozzer one of my two remaining five-pound notes.

'Cheers pal,' Yozzer inserted the note and started to push the flashing buttons. I watched the wheels spin, not really paying attention to how they ended up, 'Yes, come on!' Yozzer exclaimed as he got onto the board. In my pocket, my phone vibrated. Alicia responding. At the back of my mind, I wondered if you'd heard and one of these texts would be from you. Wishful thinking, I guess.

'I know babe, but I'll see you Friday xxx.'

I decided against replying for now, a little annoyed that I wasn't able to go around. Yozzer noticed the phone in my hand.

'Do we need to go onto phone rules?' he asked, watching the fruit machine carefully.

'I'm not replying. She's too busy to see me tonight.'

'Well I've got no plans, we can just get pissed if you want, call in sick tomorrow.'

'That's taking the Mick a little bit, innit?'

Yozzer turned to face me for a moment 'We just read our best mate's suicide note. I dunno about you, but all I wanna do now is get messed up.'

'I could do with taking the edge off things, I suppose,' I nodded.

'OK, well I could give Mark a call, if you want,' Yozzer lowered his voice. Mark was Yozzer's dealer. I hadn't done cocaine in a while, it always made me a bit shitty the next day, but right now I really didn't care. In fact, I think the last time was when you and I got a gram and stayed up all night at yours after a particularly tough game.

'Yeah, All right.'

'Here,' Yozzer put his hand in his pocket, looking over to make sure the barman wasn't watching. He wasn't, so Yozzer slipped a small baggy into my hand 'there's a couple of lines left in that, go and have one for now and I'll call Mark, FUCKING YES!'

Yozzer pressed the 'Collect' and pound coins started to pour into the change slot, thirty of them to be exact. About thirteen pounds up overall, not bad. I went to the toilet as Yozzer went to change the coins into notes at the bar.

I went into the only cubicle and locked the door behind me. I sat on the toilet seat, lid down and balanced my phone on my knees. Then I took out my wallet and the baggy, pouring a small amount of the white powder onto my phone screen. It was already pretty ground up. I placed the last fiver I had flat over the top and crushed the rest of the powder by sweeping my debit across the note. I know I didn't need to, but it was habit from when we did it because you never ground it up properly!

I wiped any powder off the note onto the phone screen to join the rest the coke. I used the debit card to line the coke up, rolled up the note and, being positive no one had entered the loos, snorted the line.

I'd missed it. I really had. The coke hit the back of my throat and the rush was almost instantaneous, probably because it had been so long since I'd touched the stuff. With my finger I wiped the remnants of cocaine off my phone screen and rubbed it into my gums. Then I stood up, wiped my nose with the back of my hand, sniffing to get any loose bits, and left the toilets. Yozzer was sat down at a table away from the bar, a fresh pint in front of him and one next to my half-finished smooth. I approached him and under the table slipped him the baggy back.

'Mark can sort us a half each, forty quid,' Yozzer said in a lowered tone. I took the dregs of my drink and finished it off, then sipped on the new one.

'Get me two,' I said, sniffing quietly.

'Two?'

'You heard.'

'You wanna do a gram tonight?'

'I want half tonight, and then half in the week, if I need it.'

'You sure?' Yozzer looked at me and I stared straight back at him. The coke was kicking in quickly and my gums and lips were going numb. I'd missed that sensation. Do you still do it?

'Yes.'

'All right, I'll text him. He's gonna come to mine in a couple of hours, he's working late.'

We sat in silence for a few minutes before Yozzer got up to go to the toilet, more than likely go and do a line himself. Whilst he was gone, I took my phone out, still with a tiny amount of coke smeared across the screen that I discreetly wiped up with my finger and rubbed into my gums. Then I looked at the message from Alicia. Seriously, what was she up to every night this week then? Seeing friends? She would have said 'seeing friends' though, surely?

Working? She never worked past six o'clock, even on busy days.

Maybe she was seeing someone else. Was she really that type of girl? I mean, people cheat after years, don't they? I'd only known Alicia a couple of months, technically not even had 'the conversation' so were we even official? Was I allowed to call her my girlfriend now? Did I have to ask? So, if she was seeing someone else was, she allowed to? She said she was falling in love with me. She could have lied. What do you think? Am I being overly paranoid?

'What you up to this week then? Xxx,' I texted her.

Problem with texting is that the person reading the message might read it in a completely different tone than when you sent it. We had a massive argument once because you thought I was having a go at you about something trivial. So Alicia might have read that as aggressive. I didn't mean it to be. Maybe I shouldn't have sent it...

I slipped my phone back into my pocket as Yozzer came back from the bathroom, twitching his nose.

'Fucking rocket fuel, this,' he said, 'sure you want two halves?'

'Yes, I want two halves,' I said.

'All right, all right, I just know it's been a while since you last did bag.'

'Don't worry about me, pal.'

'But I do,' Yozzer said and I looked up at him, 'and you know full why I care. Swifty never told anyone and I only found out about you by accident.'

'Yeah, I know mate, I'm sorry.'

'Don't apologise,' Yozzer leaned forward and rested his elbows on the table 'just know that if you wanna talk about anything, anything at all, Swifty, Alicia, Phoenix, the fucking weather, I'm here for you.'

'Thanks pal. I appreciate that. Honestly.'

'Does Alicia know?'

'Know what?' I asked, taking my beer to drink, already craving another line of cocaine. Damn, I'd missed it so much.

'That you're depressed.'

I nodded my head.

'Then don't worry. She should understand if you have any moments.'

'I'm not sure she does.'

'Why?'

I shrugged.

'I'm sure she does mate. She seems decent. Now come on, let's get on it.'

We drank the rest of our drinks and went home. I've nipped home and written all this out for you. I'm about to get smashed, so God knows if I'll remember tomorrow and I wanted to tell you about my day. Anyway, I'd better get off to meet back with Yozzer.

Jamie.

***

St Helens, June 20th *June 21st, Early hours*

Comedown Status:	Imminent
Feeling of regret:	Too many
Chance of sleeping:	Small
Work:	Probably not

Dear Shona,

I've not long gotten in. I'm still pretty coked up. It's helped sober me up, which means I am able to sit down and write you this letter. Do you really want to hear about what happened tonight? To be honest, I don't care. This letter you more than likely won't get sent anyway, even if I get round to sending the others to you. I'll probably wake up tomorrow and tear it up.

I went back to Yozzer's via a cash point. The buzz from the coke was starting to wear off, so I couldn't wait to get another line inside me. At Yozzer's we cracked open a couple of Buds and turned on his Xbox. I wondered how cocaine would affect my FIFA gameplay. Apparently, it improved it. Performance enhancing drugs and all that. First game, I battered him four-nil as Barcelona against his weak Liverpool team. He was always Liverpool if we didn't press random team select. I'd either go with Barce or PSG or someone like that. Remember when we played. You picked Palermo on the basis they played in pink.

At full time, there was a knock on Yozzer's front door. Delivery man was here. Mark came in wearing a yellow parka coat with fur around the hood. He couldn't look more like a drug dealer if he tried. Seen too many films when high, I reckon.

'All right lads, three halves, yeah?' he said, pulling out a cigarette tin he carried the merchandise around in.

'Yes please, mate,' Yozzer said rubbing his hands.

'I'll do you a deal then pal, three for a hundred,' Mark tossed three small baggies full of coke onto the coffee table in the middle of the room.

'Sound mate, you absolute legend!' Yozzer handed him five crisp twenty-pound notes.

'How you doing anyway, Yozzer?' Mark asked, counting the money and then shoving it into his pocket. I wasn't paying attention anymore. I'd pulled my phone out to read and reply to Alicia's latest message.

'I've got a lot on, seeing my friends, you'll see me Friday xxx.'

Seemed a little off to me, what do you think? She said friends, but she could be lying. Plus all week? I get her best friends will be up there, but she couldn't re-arrange seeing other friends cause I need her? I was being neurotic and paranoid and a little selfish, and I knew it. Then again, how many times has someone close to her lost their best friend to the same illness that they've got? Was I being selfish? I wondered if you would have cancelled plans for me if you were still in my life. I bet you would. But I suppose with Alicia it had only been a week.

'Could I not come see you after you've seen your mates? Xxx,' was what I wrote back. Probably the wrong thing to say but hey, I was getting smashed.

'Here y'are, knobhead,' Yozzer said, handing me two of the bags and a tenner. 'Only fair we split that twenty quid Mark has saved us.'

'Cheers,' I said, taking them and grabbing the empty FIFA case, ready to grind up the coke. I could see a couple of big rocks in one of the bags, so it had to be done.

'Have a good night lads. Yozzer, call me if you need anything,' Mark got up to leave and embraced Yozzer before going. I ground up all the coke together in the same manner I had at The Wheatsheaf and split the now fine powder into two piles, one for tonight and one for later in the week. Using the tenner that I had folded in half, I poured the coke back into their bags, except for one line, which I did then and there. I handed the empty case to Yozzer. He does his different to me. He crushes any rocks inside the bag, but he liked the make a line and grind it at the same time, then snort it. At home that's cool, but out it's a bit of a ball-ache. That's why I liked to prep mine.

'Woah, Moma!' Yozzer cried, pulling his head up, his eyes wide, 'rocket fuel, I tell thee!'

'Fucking A, mate!' I said. I was alert now, ready to go. Still paranoid, maybe more so, but energetic.

'One more game?'

'Go on then!'

We played a fast and frantic game. Every replay was skipped and all free kicks were rushed. The precision had gone, replaced instead with a need to score a goal as soon as possible. I won again, because Yozzer was shit, this time though he did bag a goal, and it ended four-one. I know you like football so that's why I'm telling you the scores, even though it's not important. Maybe it is. Maybe I'm still coked up. I checked my phone as Yozzer turned off the console and we got up to leave. Alicia hadn't replied yet. I reckon she was ignoring me. I didn't check the blue ticks.

'Back to The Wheatsheaf?' Yozzer suggested.

'Nah, I'm too buzzed for there, Punch?'

'Yeah I could go Punch.'

We left Yozzer's and walked to the Punch Tarmey, where the only thing we drank was Guinness. What else would you drink there? I paid with card, as I wanted to keep my notes to use for the coke, which I did a line of pretty much as soon as we got there.

I did another line half an hour later.

By now my heart were going like the clappers. I could feel I was grinding my teeth already and every time I made myself aware of this I was able to stop. I didn't want anyone to know what I were doing, especially staff, or we'd be barred and I loved this place. Am I writing this too quick? Can you keep up? My phone buzzed as I licked the screen after doing the second line, which I'm not gonna lie scared the crap outa me. It was Alicia, finally replying to me.

'No Jamie. I have work early each morning. I'll see you Friday. Xxx.'

OK, now she was pissed. She never usually used full stops in text messages like that. Did she? I couldn't remember. Maybe she did. Did it matter? Punctuation and that, in a text? The coke was playing havoc with my brain, I couldn't think straight. Even now I don't know if she did or not. I tried to think back to your messages when you were pissed at me. Yep, you always put full stops when you were angry. I just typed out a response.

'I wouldn't stay long, just see you xxx.'

Was that too needy? I had every right to be needy. My best friend had just hung himself. I'd just read how unhappy he was. I thought I had every right to be a little needy. You understand. The reply was almost instant.

'No Jamie. Xxx.'

Damn, that were really short. Short messaging time it was. 'Fine.'

No kisses, no nothing. Shoulda put kisses. Now she'll think I'm being a dick. Ahh, sod it, she was being a bitch. You hated it when I dropped the kisses.

'You all right, pal?' I looked up from my phone to see a middle-aged bloke walking towards the urinals but looking at me intensely. I realised I was stood in the middle of the men's room, clutching my phone with two hands quite tightly. Too tightly.

'Aye, yeah, I'm right,' I said, putting my phone away and leaving the toilets to return to Yozzer.

'All good?' Yozzer asked. Two shots of tequila and a wedge of lime were sat in front of us as well as two fresh pints of Guinness. Just what I needed right now. I hadn't eaten anything in a few hours and the coke was staving off my appetite. And now tequila? Fine.

'Yeah mate, these ours?'

'Well they aint Swifty's,' Yozzer said. I looked at him and raised my eyebrows, 'Oh come on, we're a bit hammered and Swifty wouldn't want us grieving every second of the day. He'd want us joking and smiling. He'd find it funny!'

'You're right. Bottoms up,' we downed the tequila's in unison and sucked on the lime. I hated tequila. Though it did remind me of the time you let me do a body shot off you in that Mexican bar in Manchester. Remember that? Great night that was.

'All right, my turn,' Yozzer got up and went to the bathroom. I opened the text conversation with Alicia. Of course, no response to that dickhead message, so I typed back 'I'm sorry xxx,' and decided to leave it. Yozzer returned quite quickly and we drank our pints.

'Wanna play snooker?' Yozzer suddenly asked.

'Snooker?'

'Yeah, we could go Scala.'

'Where's that?'

'Above Iceland.'

'I'm coked off my tits.'

'So?'

'Yeah all right, let's go play some snooker!'

We downed our pints and left. The snooker hall weren't too far from Punch Tarmey, though our walking pace now was closing in on Olympic power walking standard. We were able to secure a table and I left Yozzer to rack up whilst I went and did another line in the toilets, but some arsehole was in the cubicle. Instead, I pretended to take a piss at the urinal and checked my phone.

No new messages.

I went back out and over to our table that Yozzer had expertly set up. I hadn't played snooker in time though. Yozzer played it a bit, he were pretty good to be fair to him, so I let him break. Still, would have been a fun place for us to come. I'm sure you don't like being reminded how I used to beat you at pool. Snooker was really not the right sport to be playing whilst high on cocaine however. I kept over-hitting the balls. Yozzer laughed every time, because even though he was coked off his face as well, he was still able to it with the right force. He started to go on a bit of a break, so I checked my phone yet again.

Still no messages.

The little blue tick said she'd read it though.

For God's sake, I said sorry, what more does she want? She was taking the piss, right?

'Come on, I said sorry, didn't mean to be a dick xxx.'

'Oi, dickhead, put your fucking phone away it's your go,' Yozzer called over, as a red ball slowed down to a stop in the middle of the table. The pink was off its spot and there were a few reds scattered around. The rest of the colours were where they started. You must know what a starting snooker table looks like.

'How many you get?' I asked, sliding my phone into my back pocket.

'Forty-two, not bad.'

'Get us a round in, Guinness.'

'All right, but no cheating.'

Yozzer headed off to the bar and I examined the table. The white ball had found itself in a good position just to the left of the blue. There was a red near the corner pocket, so I lined up the shot and took it. I hit the cue ball far too hard, but the angle was just right so the red went in. The white ricocheted into a group of three reds near the black and somehow I had a straight shot on the black into the opposite corner. I took it on, and I was able to cue the white back to be onto a red. I was quite impressed with myself. You would have been as well. It looked good. Yozzer returned with two pints and he placed them on a nearby table.

'Did you just get the black?'

'Yes mate, and now I'm on for that red in the same pocket!'

'Well replace it then,' Yozzer took a good couple of gulps of the Black Stuff. I took the black ball out of the rail of the corner pocket and put it back on its spot. Then I lined up on the red that was on. It had a slight angle, but I still put it in. My placement game wasn't the best though, so I realised I didn't have a colour set up next. The thing with snooker, Shona, is you have to think ahead. I chalked up my cue and thought about what I was going to go for. The blue looked like the best option, so I just went for it in the middle pocket.

Nowhere near.

'Mate you need to slow down.'

'Slow down?!' I opened my eyes wide and stared over at Yozzer.

'Yeah, you're rushing your shots.'

'I couldn't slow down if you dropped a Valium in me pint!'

'Watch me,' Yozzer lowered his head above his cue and took a shot on that to me looked quite difficult; A red in the corner at a nearly ninety-degree angle. He struck the ball oh so delicately and the red dropped in. I looked at my phone for the umpteenth time today but of course there were no new messages.

'Fine, be like that.'

I'll probably regret that one as well, when she finally gets back to me. She never replied to me tonight.

Yozzer beat me. Of course he did, I don't think there was any hope in Hell that I was gonna win. He re-racked, I had another line in the bogs and this time I broke. Nowhere near as good as his though, I completely left him on and he started potting balls left right and centre, literally. Still no response, but another blue tick next to the message. She was reading the damn things. She could at least reply to something.

Or maybe she was with her new lover.

Or she just didn't care.

I tried calling her, but she didn't answer. It was getting late now, time seemed to be flying past and I knew why. Yozzer beat me again and this time I didn't pot a single ball. I was far too hammered by this point. I got us one more round in and we gave the snooker balls back. After that drink, we left. Though Yozzer had offered I could stay at his, I decided to just come home. I wanted to pass out on my own bed. On the walk back, after Yozzer and I had split, I tried calling Alicia again.

Still no answer.

Now I'm sat here writing this letter. And I've just noticed it's after midnight, I'd better change the date at the top. I remembered the coke in my pocket. The baggy I had had today was empty, so I tore it open and gummed the remnants, my mouth pretty much still completely numb from the last lot I'd done. The other half gram I tossed onto my bedside table. I checked my phone. Still no response. I tried calling again. No answer. I plugged in the charger and undressed. I got an overwhelming urge to call you. Thank God I have deleted your number. Have you deleted mine as well?

Jamie.

P.S. That coke is really good, you should get some.

***

St Helens Town Centre, June 21st

Hours Slept:	7ish
Dreams:	Lurid
Antidepressants:	None
Breakfast:	Not Today
Gym:	Probably Not

Dear Shona,

First thing I did today when I woke up was re-read that letter I wrote last night. More than likely won't be sending you that one. The next thing I did was check my phone.

'We need to talk x.'

That was the text from Alicia sent at around 6.30am. I'm guessing when she woke up. Shit. I had vague memories of what I'd been sending so I re-read the conversation.

Shitty shit.

I tried calling her as well, didn't I? I fell back onto my bed with my head in my hands as I contemplated what the best course of action was. I would have to meet up with her but she was busy until Friday. I had to handle this well. You can decide on whether I did or didn't. My head was pounding. Damn cocaine, I knew last night that I would regret it. I typed a message out and then read it back to myself out loud.

'I'm so sorry Alicia, I ended up getting really drunk and it was a tough day, I can't remember calling you or sending these messages, I'm honestly so sorry xxx.'

Was that all right? Hopefully she would realise that it wasn't me last night. You probably won't get to read what I got up to, as I doubt I'll send the letter, basically I was a complete dickhead and acted in a way that just wasn't like me at all. Alicia knew the real me. At least I hope she did. This is the real reason we took the phones off each other when we were out. So that we didn't do stupid shit like this. I didn't even like the person I was when I was coked up. You would have hated him as well. Damn drugs and alcohol, one or the other Taz, for God's sake.

I checked the time. Quarter past seven. I could have called in sick; the boss would understand. But then what would I do? Stare at the ceiling again? No, no I couldn't spend my days doing that, no matter how much my head hurt. A Berocca and a shower and I'd be right. I'd slept naked, probably because I was sweating like a Gypsy in the tax office, so I grabbed my towel off the radiator and went into the bathroom. The water felt like liquid gold as I stuck my head under the shower. I pressed my hands against the wall and let the water hit the top of my head and run down my body. I stood there for a lot longer than I intended before I washed my hair. Then I rubbed some shower gel over my body and let the water rinse it off. Alicia had replied by the time I was finished.

'Meet me for lunch at one in town. You can't message me like that x.'

It read so ominously. I messaged back agreeing then sat for ten minutes, leaning on my knees, my hands clasped together. I was such an asshole. Finally, I stood up, dressed, sorted out my hair and went into work.

All morning I thought about what Alicia was going to say to me. Was she going to dump me, was she going to have a go, was going to confirm my paranoia? I was working so slowly, I barely got anything done, so the morning dragged. When lunch finally rolled around I had done bugger all. Alicia had said Café Nero in town, which would help, I could use some caffeine to shift this hangover/comedown.

'I was with Jen last night, Jamie. And you're sending me messages making me feel shitty,' Alicia said as she sat down with a large mocha. Same as you. I had a large cappuccino, as per.

'Why didn't you tell me you were with Jen?' I asked.

'Because it shouldn't matter who I was with or what I was doing, you can't be sending me messages like that.'

'You're right, I know, I'm sorry.'

'Are you?'

'Of course I am!'

'Look, Jamie, I know this is a tough time for you,' Alicia leaned forward and took my hand 'and I know you struggle. But you can't take it out on me.'

'That's not what I was doing, Alicia.'

'Then what is it? I don't want to be getting message after message and call after call whilst I'm with my friends.'

'I needed you. I've just lost me best mate and I needed my girl!'

'I can't imagine what that is like,' Alicia admitted.

'That's all it was.'

'But you can't rely on me, Jamie. You can't rely on me for your happiness, I can't be your crutch.'

'So what are you saying, are you dumping me?'

'See, that's just like you, assuming things. No, I'm not dumping you. But I'm saying that you have some shit going on that you need to sort out. And I will support you, but it can't be all me. I know you don't speak to your parents, but you've got Yozzer, you've got the lads, they are your family.'

'But what about you? I need you.'

'I know, but I have my own life as well. And of course I'm going to be there for you, but you can't just keep relying on me. I can't be the one who pulls you out of this. I've agreed to see you Friday, so you need to find what else works in the meantime.'

'Friday just seemed like such a long time away,' I looked down at the floor.

'It's a week Jamie. Who were you with last night?'

'Yozzer.'

'There you go. Your other best mate who I bet is hurting as much as you.'

'He's not like me though is he?' I asked looking up at Alicia, locking eyes with her. No one said anything as the café bustled away.

'Look Jamie. I know this is difficult for you. But don't let it come between us. Just know I'm not trying to distance myself from you. I meant what I said last week. But don't message me like that, OK?'

'That wasn't me,' I said.

'What do you mean, "it wasn't you"?'

'I just mean, I mean I wasn't acting like me.'

'Just please don't do it again. I'm going out for dinner with work tonight, tomorrow I said I go to my mum's and Thursday the girls are coming over. I don't want my phone going off or I'll have to turn it off.'

'I'm sorry.'

'Stop saying that! I know you're sorry. Just prove that to me by sorting yourself out. What if work need to get hold of me, or my mum or something happens and I've turned my phone off cause you won't stop messaging me?'

'You could just block my number…'

'Yes, but I don't want to do that either. I get yesterday was tough so you got drunk, but maybe lay off the booze for a bit?'

'Yeah, OK, I won't drink anymore this week.'

'Go to the gym, you haven't been since Swifty died.'

'I will.'

For a second time neither of said anything. You know she was right. I hadn't been. And you know how much I love that place. Alicia checked her watch.

'I have to get back to work. *I'LL* message you later, OK?'

'OK.'

'OK?' Alicia leaned in, repeating herself as trying to drill the message into my brain.

'Yes, OK, I won't message until you do.'

'Have a good day, babe.'

Alicia kissed me on the cheek and left. I sat back in my chair and thought about what she'd said. I was a bit annoyed, but she had a point. Just wish she had realised I wasn't *relying* on her; I just knew it's what I *needed*. Sometimes. Not all the time, just sometimes. I came home again after messaging the boss to say that I needed to grab something. Bit of a lie I wrote this letter instead. I guess I want your opinion. Am I being selfish? What do you think? How would you have reacted. I tried to think back to the last time you told me I was suffocating you. You said it a few times. To be fair though, you didn't know I was depressed. I didn't know I was. Here's the thing. I reckon you would have dropped everything if you known and I needed you. You really loved me. You really cared about me. Care about me? I hope you still do. I'd better get back to work.

Jamie.

***

Olympia Gym, St Helens, Still June 21st

Mood:	Angry
Tea:	A little bit of chicken
TV:	Naff all on
Beers:	A couple

Dear Shona,

Wasn't going to write anything again today but I thought I'd better tell you about what happened at the gym. It kind of follows on from the meeting with Alicia earlier. I got there at about six, as I stayed a little later at work to make up for going home at lunch. Fortunately the gym wasn't busy. Derek was in, squatting so much I could see the bar bending across his shoulders. I had already decided I was gonna do a full body workout, which included squats, but first bench press. I call it the 'Old School Workout' because it was the first session I used to do at the gym as teenager. It involved bench press, squats, bicep curls and weighted sit ups.

Both benches weren't in use when I got there, which made life easier. It meant I could jump straight into the workout. I did twenty reps without any weight on to warm up and open up my chest, then I popped a twenty-kilogram plate on each side. Sod it, I might as well go for it today. I had had two fat burners before I came to the gym, plus the caffeine from the large coffee earlier was still in my system, so I was buzzing with energy and was able to rep out twelve easily. The come-down from last night had gone. Without much rest, I threw on an extra five kgs each side and did another ten reps. Then

I swapped those fives for tens and did eight reps, struggling a bit on the last. I'm telling you, I'm stronger than when you last saw me.

'Want a spot?' Derek came over, removing a weightlifting belt from his waist.

'Aye, go on mate,' I replied. This was great, now I could go really heavy and go for a personal best. We swapped the tens on each side for twenties. This meant the total weight of the bar was one hundred kilograms. I repped out five easily. At this point, it felt like today could be the day.

'What's your best one rep max?' Derek asked.

'One-twenty.'

'OK, let's do that then go for one-thirty.'

I did one-twenty with Derek pushing me. He grabbed two five-kilogram plates and put them on each end. I sat up on the bench and prepared myself, breathing deeply. I thought of you watching me.

'All right mate, in your own time, you got this,' Derek said, positioning himself behind me, ready to help the bar off the rack. One hand at a time I gripped the bar and arched my back, 'OK, let's count down, ready? Three, two, one…'

I took the weight of the bar as Derek helped it up. My arms started to shake as I quickly lowered it in an effort to help bounce it straight back up. Lowering it slowly would have been a mistake. Damn it was heavy. You've no idea. It touched my breast bone and I started to push. Slowly it moved upwards.

'Come on, Taz, come on! This is all you, I ain't holding nothing!' Derek yelled. I was yelling myself, making groans as I willed the bar upwards. My face felt like it was going to burst open as blood rushed around. I wasn't thinking of you anymore. I was concentrating so hard. But something was wrong. It shifted an inch or two up but was refusing to go any further.

'Come… on…' I groaned.

'Come on Taz, keep pushing, come on!'

But it was no use. The bar didn't budge. Derek gave me a few more seconds before he took the weight and lifted it back onto the rack.

'Fuck!' I slapped the bench as I stood up, frustrated, angry.

'It's all right, always tough and you haven't trained in a couple of weeks.'

'Damnit!'

'Don't get angry mate…'

I'm ashamed to say I snapped. I through my water bottle across the gym and it hit the water fountain. A couple of people looked over at me.

'Hey! Calm down!' Derek said, approaching me. He looked even bigger when he was angry. I stared at him breathing deeply 'call it a day buddy. I heard about your mate, so I'm gonna let this slide. But don't fuck about. Go home. Relax.'

I went home after that. I'm still angry now. More so because of how I reacted. You would have been so ashamed of me. I'm ashamed of me. I really don't know what's going through my head at the moment Shona. I really don't, I don't know what to do about anything, about Alicia. I wish we were still together. Maybe none of this would be happening. Maybe.

Jamie.

***

Alicia's House, June 24th

Bottles Drank:	15
Cans:	18
Workouts:	0
Bad Dreams:	3
Test injected:	400mg
Grams Bought:	3

Dear Shona,

Things have been gotten pretty bad. And I've lost her. Alicia, I've lost her. I don't know what to do. Things are just getting shitter and shitter. I can barely hold back the tears. Crying again. What a man I am, hey? Here's what happened.

The rest of the week followed the same pattern. I would get back from work and crack open a bottle or can of beer. I'd order a Chinese from downstairs and pick it up around half seven, eight o'clock. After dinner I'd do a few lines. After a bit of persuasion Yozzer eventually gave me Mark's number and I bought three grams of coke off him, which he gave me in six baggies, a half in each. I ground it up like always, but only used three bags. I gummed the other three. I did my best not to message Alicia (any more than usual) but this morning I saw I'd sent four unanswered messages.

'How was your day today? Xxx'

'Have a good night with the girls xxx.'

'Hope your night is good xxx xx.'

'I Miss yoU x xx x.'

No response. Not even first thing this morning. I'd agreed

to go to hers right after work, and she hadn't cancelled on me, so at this point I assumed it was still on

Work was shit. Everyone just wanted it to be the weekend. I guess it's the same for you. How is work, by the way? I realise I haven't even asked. The lads and lassies in sales seemed to take things easy as well. I was told when they hit their targets or something by Thursday then Friday was a doddle for them. Sometimes, warehouse and sales go for drinks, but I never get pissed on a Friday. Well, usually I don't. At lunch I went to the pub and had a couple of pints and throughout the day I snuck to the toilets to do a key of coke. The boss thought I was working hard. If he only knew, hey? I told you things have gotten bad. At five I left and drove round to Alicia's. I could tell the moment the door opened that she was pissed.

'Come in,' she said. 'Sit down, we need to talk. Again.'

I walked through, head down, like a naughty schoolboy summoned to the head's office. I sat on her sofa and leant forward on my knees. With my hands clasped together I looked at the floor.

'Drink?' Alicia asked.

'Yes, please.'

'Have you drunk anything today?'

'I had a couple at lunch, y'know, Friday pub lunch. Why?'

'Because, Jamie, I'm worried about you.'

'Why?'

'Because I care about you! What kind of a stupid question was that?'

I shrugged.

'Jamie. You can't drink this away.'

'I know.'

'Do you? Because you did it again last night. I told you that I can't have you message me like that and look what happened. You were drunk, weren't you.'

'Yeah,' I couldn't look at her. I looked at anywhere but her. The clock on the wall, the flowers on the windowsill, a little porcelain figurine on the mantlepiece.

'Be honest, how much have you drunk this week?' She sat down next to me. Now it felt more personal. I wasn't about to get detention.

'Honestly?'

'Yes. Tell me the truth, how much?'

'A lot.'

'How much is a lot?'

'I don't know, a lot is just, a lot!'

'All right, calm down. Here's the thing, I'm gonna make you dinner, and I want to open a bottle of wine with you, but I'm scared you're going to get drunk and... well I don't know what.'

'You think I'm going to hit ya?' I finally looked up and made eye contact. She looked concerned; I'll give her that.

'Maybe. I don't know.'

'You seriously think that of me? I'm a woman beater?' I started to get angry. It was like a someone had flicked the switch. So damn ironic. You know I'm not the angry sort or that I'd ever hit a woman. Right? But I got angry at the accusation. I blame the drugs

'See! You're getting mad at the thought.'

'I'm getting mad cause you're accusing me of being a wife beater!'

'You're still getting mad!'

I took a few seconds, then I said 'Alicia, I'm not going to

hit you. I love you.'

She went silent. That was not the right time to say that. To be honest, I'm not even sure why I said it. Look at me, I'm still writing these letters to you and yet I'm telling another woman I love her. I must have felt it somewhere. I'm not a liar. It just came out. At this moment you actually flashed into my mind. Is it possible to love you and her at the same time? I'm real messed up, aren't I?

'Jamie, I can't say it back, not just yet. Not after this week. That doesn't mean I'm not still falling or care, but I feel if I say it now, I'm just saying it to comfort you. Then you're going to need me every single day and I can't handle that right now. I couldn't handle it earlier in the week, I couldn't do it much more.'

I don't know what feeling I was expecting to feel. Maybe a sniper shot straight to the chest. But it wasn't that. I honestly didn't feel anything. I wasn't hurting, I wasn't in pain, I was just, what do you reckon, numb? It's hard to break a heart that's already shattered.

'So you don't love me.'

'Come on. You know what my feelings are. And I only think you're saying that because of how low you are. You *need* that love, and you're just saying it. Maybe Swifty left a hole and you're filling it.'

'Of course he left a hole!'

'Then don't just fill it with me! Look, I care so much about you, I really do. But this, it's not there yet and I think you know that too.'

I said nothing. I didn't know what to say. My brain had frozen. It's the hole you left as well. I couldn't tell Alicia that though, could I? Then she'd think she was a rebound. Couple that with the Swifty shaped hole that was gaping, maybe I was just saying it because I needed to hear someone say it to me. Reminds me of the time I got you to say it to me when we were having sex. I need that reassurance, even in those sorts of situations. Right now, I needed to hear it from Alicia.

'Let's have some pasta, a bottle of wine, just one bottle, watch a movie and relax. You've got a game tomorrow, yeah?' Alicia said.

'Yeah, an away game.'

'OK, well then tonight we can chill. Watch something shit.'

'OK. Yeah, OK that sounds good.'

Alicia kissed me, stood up and went through to the kitchen. From my pocket I took out my keys, phone and wallet and put them on the coffee table. Alicia returned, two glasses of red wine in her hands. She handed one of them to me and I took a sip. Then she went to put my stuff on the side.

'Here, let me put this through in the hallway so it's out of the way,' she said. As she picked up my wallet, the bag of cocaine fell out onto the floor. I made a move to grab it but Alicia picked it up first, 'Jamie, what is that?'

'I can explain that.'

'Well you'd better fucking start!'

I had no explanation. She hates this stuff.

'Jamie? Come on, explain it.'

Nothing.

'What did I say last week? When I found your steroids, what did I say? If you were on drugs we had a problem and this is a big problem!'

'It's helped,' was all I could manage.

'Helped?! It's cocaine, Jamie! When did you start taking this shit?' She was shouting now, almost screaming.

'I got it when I was with Yozzer. I needed something to take the edge off everything.'

'You're having a laugh. You *must* be kidding me! Take the edge off it?'

'Well you weren't there for me, were you?' I went on the offensive. It was the wrong tactic, but I didn't know how else to deal with it. I couldn't stand her having a go.

'Excuse me?!'

'You were too busy with you friends and work people, more important than your struggling boyfriend!'

'Jamie! I have my own life. I can't drop it all for you! I told you, you can't just use me as a crutch!'

'Well I didn't did I?'

'That didn't mean go and start shoving your problems up your nose!'

'It did the trick!'

'I'm getting rid of this,' Alicia walked towards the door, but I stood quickly and blocked her path, 'Get out of my way, Jamie.'

'Give me the bag,' I said, my hand out in front of her, palm open.

'Move, Jamie, now.'

'Give me the bag,' I repeated, my voice cold, purposeful, my eyes staring through her. You'd never seen me like this. 'I won't ask again.'

'Well, I guess we know what is important to you,' Alicia slaps the bag down into my palm. I went to my wallet and slid the bag back into it. From behind me, Alicia spoke again, 'I don't think I can do this anymore.'

'Do what?' I looked over my shoulder at her.

'This. You. I can't handle it.'

'Alicia, what are you saying?' I placed the wallet down and tilted my head as I walked to her.

'I'm saying I can't do it anymore. I'm really not strong enough for a dependant relationship. This has been a real strain on us, on me.'

'A strain on you? How do you think it's been on me?'

'I know, and that's what's made it difficult. The coke, the phone calls, the messages, the dependency, the expectation, it's all too much for me.'

'Are you dumping me?'

'I... don't know if I can do it.'

'Yeah, you've said that already. Are you dumping me?'

'Yes, I think I am. I have to think about myself, or it's just going to destroy us both.'

I stared at her. I didn't know what to say. I could hear the clock ticking by slowly, each tick lasting far longer than a second. Then I said; 'Don't do this, Alicia.'

'Jamie, I'm sorry, but this has to happen. I was thinking about doing it before you came over, but I thought I'd give you one last chance. But now I know about the coke, and the steroids. You need to sort yourself out, and I can't be there until you do.'

'Alicia, don't. I need you to be there. I can sort myself out, I'm not acting like myself.'

'I know you're not, but until you are, I can't be here. What you're doing, the way you are behaving, it makes me angry. And when I'm angry it pulls on our relationship. And that is toxic for you *and* me.'

'Alicia, please, please. Come on, I'm sorry, I can sort this out, I promise, I'm sorry,' I was panicking and that was making me beg. Worst thing I could do.

'I think you should go Jamie,' Alicia looked away.

'Alicia, please,' I reached out and clawed at her arm, but she pulled it away.

'Please, just go Jamie, I need some space.'

'Come on, we can work on this,' I was desperate, still pawing at her sleeves.

'Jamie, don't do this. You're making it worse, just go home,' she stepped past me and rubbed her eye. A tear?

'Alicia…'

'I need some space from you,' she said, her back to me. She couldn't even look at me.

'There is someone else, isn't there?' I asked, not even sure I wanted to hear the answer. I don't know where that came from either. I just blurted it out.

'See! There you go again! I've told you, no!' she was mad. She turned around to face me. If she was about to cry, she wasn't now.

'Just seems a little, not like you, really, to end things like this.'

'For God's sake, Jamie, I've tried to explain! And you jump to conclusions. No. There isn't anyone else. I just need some space!' I stared at her again, breathing a little shaky and short. She looked away again, unable to get eye contact.

'Fine. I'll go,' and I left. I drove straight home, opened a bottle of beer and racked up a line the size of a damn teaspoon. I drank and I drank, and I snorted and I snorted. I sent some texts to Alicia. She never replied. I did the entire gram of cocaine and a load of beers. Then I wrote this letter. I can't stand being alone. When I write to you, it's like you are here and once again Shona I need you. I need you to tell me it's all going to be OK. I need you to hold me close and play with my hair in that way you used to. The way that used to calm me down and made me feel safe. I needed that now more than ever.

Jamie.

***

Ashton Bears v Sutton Phoenix, June 25th

Hours Slept:	Not Enough
Breakfast:	None
Pre-Game Fat Burners:	7
Headache:	Massive
Mood:	Lowest it could be

Dear Shona,

The game didn't go well for me at all. I've come back for a bit and I'm supposed to be going back out when Yozzer gets here. I don't want to go. But once I've had some more coke I'll be right. Thought I'd come and tell you about the game first.

I woke up after twelve. I groaned, grabbed my face and felt like crying again. All I wanted to do was go back to sleep. My stomach felt like there was a Slayer concert going on in there; people moshing around, with no idea what was going on. My head was performing constant triple axels, and my mouth was dry. The feeling of regret was intense. I checked my phone but nothing from Alicia. The last three messages hadn't even been delivered; she'd blocked my number. Can't blame her. I sat on the edge of the bed and held my head in my hands. I'd slept fully clothed and I absolutely stank. My t-shirt was drenched in sweat. I peeled it off, along with the rest of my clothes. It wasn't a pretty sight. If you'd been there, you'd have left for sure.

I set the shower to lukewarm, wishing I could stay under the water forever. But I was already running late. I had to get my shit together and get over to Ashton. Kick-off was at two-thirty and I was supposed to be there a little earlier than the meet time, which was one o'clock. The warm-up started at one-thirty.

I arrived at one-twenty-five.

'Taz, you're late,' Coach said.

'I know, I know, I'm sorry I got held up.'

'Get yer boots on and get on the pitch,' he said monotonously. He was pissed. I rushed into the changing rooms and started to get my kit on. The number one jersey was hung up on a coat hanger above the bench. Yozzer came in from the physio's carrying an orange Lucozade bottle.

'Where you hell have you been?'

'Overslept,' I said, tearing off my clothes and putting on my game kit.

'You look like shit.'

'Thanks, pal.'

'Weren't you with Alicia last night?'

'Yeah. I don't wanna talk about it.'

'Everything All right?'

'I don't wanna talk about it, Yozzer!' I snapped motioning Yozzer to stop with my hand.

'Fine. See you on the pitch.'

The warm-up did nothing but antagonise my comedown. I was sluggish and slow. My sharp turns were non-existent and I dropped a couple of very catchable high balls that Yozzer put up for me. Then the game kicked off and I struggled to keep up. They scored with their first two possessions. Both times someone missed a tackle in the defensive line, but I was slow to react. They ran around me so easily and scored under the posts to take an early 12-0 lead. Then we got a scrum for a forward pass on our own twenty, for which I went at first receiver. It was a simple enough pass but I wasn't concentrating and knocked

151

the ball on as it bounced off my forearm. I lashed out at the ball with my foot and kicked it downfield, fortunately before the ref blew his whistle. We did manage to get a try before half time, with no assistance from me, Yozzer selling a dummy and scoring himself, but they scored two more, both converted, to make it 24-6.

At half time Coach and Skip gave us all a bollocking. We had been shite, but me especially. After the shouting, Skip gave us a few minutes to find our heads. That's when he approached me.

'What's going on mate?' he asked.

'Nothing, I'm fine.'

'Those were simple tackles. You were sitting too deep, and you never sit that far back. What's going on?'

'Honestly, nothing, I'm fine. Seriously, Skip, don't worry.'

'Well buck your ideas up. Coach is this close to bringing you off.'

The second half kicked off with them kicking to us. The ball dropped at around the thirty and bobbled its way towards me as I advanced from my starting position between the sticks. It was a comfortable enough gather, but I wasn't able to take it in and knocked on. Again.

'Fucking Hell, Taz!' Mac groaned from behind me. I looked at the floor, my hands on my hips. It was really poor Shona. For once, I wasn't thinking of you watching me. I was embarrassed.

'All right lads, shit happens. Make up for it now, hey Taz,' Skip said, patting my shoulder. I nodded but didn't say anything. I took my place at the back of the scrum, meaning the loose forward could join the line and help stop their big runners. But he didn't, and their big second rower barged threw and I took chase. It was only twenty metres to the try line but

I sprinted, as best I could after him. As he crossed the line he placed the ball on the ground. In my frustration, I dropped my shoulder and levelled the guy. Players came running in, grabbing my shirt, Skip trying to pull me away.

'Right, one, get here now!' The ref demanded. Skip came over with me, 'so it's a try here, then foul play in the act of scoring, it's an eight-point try and a yellow card.'

'Oh come on, sir, he's already put the ball down, it's after the try is scored!'

'Don't argue, eight-point try, full back in the bin,' the ref raised his hands above his head, signalling 'ten' towards our bench. Coach looked over with his arms folded. I'd never been yellow carded before. I trudged across the field, my head hanging, refusing to look at anyone as their half back slotted the conversion and then the penalty right in front of the sticks. Coach said nothing and I stared at the floor as I sat on the bench. After a few minutes, he sat next to me.

'That were never an eight-pointer,' I protested.

'That's not the point.'

'I know. I'll get it together when I get back on.'

'You're not going back on,' Coach said, not even looking at me.

'What?'

'I don't know where your head is at, Mac, tighten that A up!' he yelled onto the pitch, and then to me 'but it sure as hell isn't in this game.'

We lost in the end, even though we pulled two back in the second half. Just as we started a comeback and brought it to 24-18, they scored with five minutes left to make it 30-18. Yozzer dragged me upstairs after we showered, insisting I didn't go home straight away. He bought me a pint and sat me in a corner.

'So, what's going on?' he asked me.

'I told you, I'm fine.'

'Like shit you are.'

I gulped down two large mouthfuls of beer.

'Fine, don't tell me, be a miserable bastard. But I'd rather you did mate. I'd rather you told me what was going on in that head of yours.'

'Alicia dumped me last night.'

'Ahh mate…'

'Yeah. I know. She found the coke, said she couldn't deal with me like this, me needing her and all that.'

'Seriously?'

'Yeah. Said I was too much. That I shouldn't be relying on her. But it's not about relying, it's just that sometimes I need her. Not all the time, but with all that's happened, I need her more than normal.'

'That's a bit shit, mate.'

'I reckon there's someone else,' I sat back on my chair and watched some of the lads starting to prepare a drinking game.

'What's she done that's made you think that?'

'I just reckon there is,' I shrugged.

'Right pal, you're being paranoid. Yeah, that's a bit shitty cause I can see why you need her right now, so that's on her. But I know you and you think the worst.'

'Maybe.'

'If she aint strong enough to be able to deal with your depression, fuck her. That's on her pal. I know you like her…'

'I told her I loved her.'

'What did she say?'

'She said wasn't there yet.'

'Right, fuck this, Skip, yes please mate, two more on that game!'

We played Fuck the Bus and I started to loosen up a bit. I say loosen up, I started to get drunk. I snuck off a couple of times and keyed some coke, making sure Coach or no one caught me. I managed to convince Yozzer to let me go home for an hour or so. He said he'd come and get me, so I'm just waiting for him as I write to you. He should be here in a minute so I'll finish up. I'm so glad you weren't at today's game. I feel so ashamed. First ever yellow. I hope you are OK. Maybe I'll write to you when I get home.

Jamie

***

The Early Hours of June 26th

Anxiety:	Through the Roof
Head:	Drunk
Money Spent:	Too Much
Feelings:	Paranoid

Dear Shona,

I shouldn't have gone back out. Oh God, what have I done? I lost it, I really lost control. I don't know what came over me. I could be in so much trouble. I'll get straight to it.

Yozzer got me ten minutes after I finished that last letter. He thrust tequila and sambuca down me. And I kept on with the coke. We went Punch Tarmey's and by the time it was my round I was drunk. My heart was racing and my head was spinning. I ordered two Guinness's and two tequilas and as I turned around I bumped into the guy next to me, spilling the shots.

'Hey, watch it pal,' he said, wiping his arm. He wasn't much bigger than me, light ginger hair and a designer beard the same shade.

'Fuck off, you knocked them out me hand. Get us two more.'

'You what?' he squared up to me. I didn't back down.

'You heard, get us two more in, ya ginger prick,' my face was inches away from his, our noses almost touching.

'You'd better back away pal,' the ginger lad snarled.

'All right, not today, sorry mate, ignore him, he's just been dumped!' Yozzer dragged me away.

'You're a lucky cunt,' I yelled back at the lad.

'Oi!' the barmaid shouted at us.

'Sorry love, just too much, bad day, I got him,' Yozzer shoved me into a booth away from the bar. 'What the hell is wrong with you?'

'He's a wanker!' I said, waving Yozzer away from me.

'He didn't even do anything mate! I saw the whole thing!'

'He knocked our drinks out me hand and then he's starting shit!'

'You need to calm down mate!'

'I am calm!'

'Are you heckers calm! You're starting on random lads at the bar!'

'He started on me!'

'No he didn't! Jesus, Taz, maybe you should have just stayed home.'

'You're the one that dragged me out, now you're telling me to go home! Piss off Yozzer.'

'I thought you needed a night out. Thought it would take your mind off things.'

'Well it hasn't, has it? Great plan, Yozzer, I'm drunk, feel like shit, people starting on us and I'm still thinking about Swifty and Alicia and…' I stopped myself short before I said your name. He didn't need to know I've been writing these letters.

'And what?'

'Nothing, I'm just angry and heartbroken.'

'You don't need blame me though pal.'

'You don't even know what love is like, you just get by being all breezy and shit and don't get these shitty feelings!'

'Oh come off it.'

'Yeah, go off and go have another dirty one-night stand or with that slut Natalie.'

157

'Watch it mate…'

'No go on, don't have feelings or shit. Just go get laid,' I waved Yozzer away. He didn't say anything, I could just feel him staring at me. I was acting like a complete wanker, I know.

'Fine, you're on your own,' and he left. I sat there, alone, drinking the Black Stuff. The ginger lad had disappeared. I couldn't see anyone I knew. They wouldn't serve me anymore, so I left and did some cocaine in an ally, spilling some on the floor. I decided not to bother anywhere else so started walking home. That's when I clocked the ginger lad. He had parted from his friends so was walking by himself. I followed him down the road and into that ginnel a few streets away from my flat, the one going to the park.

'Oi,' I called out after him, 'oi, wanker.'

He turned around. 'Who's that?'

'Me, from the Tarmey, the tequilas.'

'Who?'

'You know 'who', me, no one around now, pal.'

'I've no idea who you are, I can't even see you,' by this point the ginger had stopped and was squinting, trying to see me through the darkness of the ally. When I approached him, I didn't break stride I just shoved him square in the chest. He reeled backwards and fell to the floor.

'Come on, ya soft cunt!' I shouted, then I grabbed him by his shirt, pulling him towards me. I rained down fist after fist. I heard his nose break under my knuckles. Blood spouted everywhere. All I could feel was rage. I think I wanted to kill him. Shit, I'm in so much trouble. I threw him down to the ground and stood over him 'think you can turn your back?' I screamed 'so much easier isn't it!'

Then Alicia's face looked up at me through the blood. My anger intensified and my nostrils flared. I swear to you, it was now Alicia looking up at me. I raised my foot and brought it crashing down onto her face. I felt the crunch beneath me as her head sandwiched between my boot and the concrete. The satisfaction mixed with rage and I stomped again. And again.

And again.

The ginger lad spluttered. His eyes were barely visible, and he spluttered blood as two teeth fell out. I breathed shortly, catching my breath. Realisation coursed across me and I ran, just as two people at the end of the ginnel appeared.

'Oi!' was all I heard as I sprinted off. I hid for twenty minutes, making sure no one had seen me, or as best I could in my state, before getting home. Oh my God, Shona, I'm in so much shit. I haven't been in a proper fight since school. I don't know what came over me. And I swear to God I saw Alicia looking at me and that made me want to stamp harder. What the hell is wrong with me?

Jamie.

***

The Wheatsheaf, St Helens, June 27th

TV Shows Watched: 7
Dreams: Overt
Instagram Posts: 0
Food Eaten: Left Over Chinese

Dear Shona,

I spent that Sunday in bed. All day. That's why I didn't write you anything. I couldn't bring myself to even get up, or look at myself in the bathroom mirror. Even today I'm feeling like shit. And I really messed up on Saturday. More than I thought or told you about. Yozzer messaged me yesterday apologising. I apologised back. That was the way we were. No matter what the falling out, we would both apologise the next day and get on with it. We've had some major, and I mean major, fallings out over the years. But we would just say sorry and get on with our lives. Friends will be your friends no matter what. We had arranged to meet for a pint after work today.

We met at The Wheatsheaf. We were frequenting it more and there is no chance of bumping into you there. Or Alicia. We shook hands and embraced simultaneously saying 'sorry' again. I got us the first round, as I think I had more to be sorry for than him and we went to our usual booth.

'What did you do after I left then?' he asked me.

'Finished my drink and went home, they wouldn't serve me anymore,' I said.

'I'm not surprised, you were smashed!'

'Yeah, yeah I really was.'

'Oh, did you hear about that bloke that got his head kicked in?'

'No,' I felt a stone being dropped in my stomach. Yozzer pulled his phone out of his pocket and started searching for something.

'Here y'are, this lad. Was walking home and someone kicked shit out of him. Look a little like that lad you started on in Punch. Good job it aint or I'd be questioning you.'

'Oh, I see…' I looked at the article Yozzer had brought up. There were two pictures, one of a guy with a bandaged face and the other a normal head shot. He had ginger hair and ginger stubble, but it certainly wasn't the guy I had started on in the bar. I don't think I've ever felt guilt like this, and I felt completely submerged in it.

'Poor lad, he's in intensive care. He can't remember what the guy looked like either, seems just like a random attack.'

'Oh my God,' I said, still looking at the picture of the guy.

'Some people are messed up, getting their jollies off of beating up people. Bet there was more than one as well.'

'You reckon?'

'Yeah, looks like one or two, surprised the poor bastard isn't in a coma!'

'Really?' I handed Yozzer back his phone, slightly relieved that it seems this guy was never going to identify me.

'Got his head stamped in, probably get a bit of brain damage.'

Another wave of guilt shot over me. How smashed was I to have got the wrong guy? Not that that was an excuse, I shouldn't have been looking for fights anyway, let alone doing what I did. Stamping on the poor lad's head, that's just sick. I hated people who did things like that and now I'm that person.

Maybe I needed some time off the booze. No game this weekend, perfect chance to relax and not touch any beers. I wish you were around. You would help me.

'Anyway, how you doing?' Yozzer brought me back into the bar.

'I'm all right,' I said.

'You spoken to Alicia?'

'No. She doesn't want to speak to me, or hear from me, mate.'

'Bloody Nora, Taz, you spend all this time sending too many texts and shit. She dumps you and suddenly you are able to give her some space?'

'That's what she wants,' I shrugged.

'Maybe when she has had a bit of space from you, she'll come back.'

'I doubt it.'

'Don't be so negative! She probably just needs a break from you. It's a tough situation.'

'I guess.'

'Don't get me wrong, the people it's worst on is you, me, and Swifty's family. Oh that reminds me, funeral is going to be on Saturday.'

'How do you know?' I asked, finally taking the second sip of my beer. I was still hungover from the weekend.

'I bumped into Swifty's mum today. She told me all arrangements have been done. Oh, and there's something else…'

'What?' I didn't like the ominous tone in Yozzer's voice.

'She wants us to be poll bearers.'

'Us?' I raised my eyebrows, half shock, half trepidation.

'Well he didn't have any brothers, did he? His dad will be one and a couple of his cousins. Oh and his uncle, I think.

But yeah, us two.'

'Yozzer, I don't know if I can do that.'

'Why not?'

'Why not? Because it means carrying our best mate's body and lowering it into a hole in the ground.'

'It's supposed to be the men closest to him.'

'Yeah, All right I get that. But still, I don't know.'

'The whole team will be there. I'll be right there beside you. Who else would Swifty want to do it?'

I thought about it for a few seconds before I said 'OK, yeah, OK I'll do it.' Jesus, what a responsibility. An honour I suppose. But Shona, it's going to be so tough. If I had your number, I would seriously look at asking you to come.

'Good,' Yozzer finished off his pint 'you want another?'

'Not tonight mate. Still hurting, you know?'

'Yeah, me too!'

I finished off my pint and went home. Well damn, tonight didn't go in the way I thought it would. I thought about that poor lad in the hospital as I channel hopped between the news and sitcoms. How could I have been so drunk, and high, that I had started on the wrong guy? It was dark as well, I suppose. Maybe I do have a bit of a problem. Only reason I haven't drank any more tonight wasn't because I'm still hurting from Saturday, but because I wanted to get home and be alone.

Swifty's family want me to be a poll bearer. I'd never done anything like it before and I suppose I wasn't going to do it for my mum and dad. It will be tough, for sure, but I think I'll struggle more watching someone else do that job. As if on cue, my phone went off. Swifty's mum, messaging me about it. Looks like Yozzer had told her he'd seen me, so I told her that it was all all right. The funeral will be at eleven on Saturday. Oh Shona, I don't know if I can do it. I don't know if I'm strong enough.

Jamie.

***

Holy Cross and Saint Helen Catholic Church, St Helens, August 1ˢᵗ

Mood:	Anxious
Gym Sessions:	4
Breakfast:	Skipped
Funeral Attendees:	50

Dear Shona,

Sorry I haven't written this week. I didn't see much point as I just did the same thing; wake up, work, gym, home, TV, sleep. But I've just got back from Swifty's funeral and I have no idea which emotion is going through me at the moment. What a send-off it was. I got through it and the wake was, well let tell you about it.

This morning I still wasn't prepared. I'd met with the other poll bearers and Yozzer on the Friday. A couple of Swifty's cousins had come over from Dublin, and we'd gone over what we had to do. Apparently, we wouldn't take too much of the weight. The undertakers would do that. It was more representational, I think.

The service was at eleven. Swifty weren't that religious but his family were. They were proper Catholics, you know. Hymns and Bible readings and all that. To be honest I was barely paying attention to what was going on. After I carried his coffin to the front of the church I just sat down and stared at the floor. Twice Yozzer had to nudge me to stand up because a hymn was about to be sung. I just opened the hymnbook at a random page. Didn't even utter a word.

Swifty's dad gave a decent eulogy. He spoke about the team, who were sat behind us, and how much he loved Phoenix. He said how good a talent he was, which was true. He spoke about how he'd always worked hard at everything he did, how at school he'd got his head down and got good grades. He spoke about how you could always rely on Swifty, and how much his friends and family loved him and will miss him. I did my best not to cry and managed to hold most of it back. Just the one tear ran down my face. I wonder if any of the rest of the team were doing the same behind me.

Holding back crying is tough. Your face feels like It's about to blow a blood vessel or something. But I did well. After the service, the rest of the poll bearers and I took the coffin out and round to the graveside. A load of people had come to say goodbye to Swifty, but only a few went to the grave. His family did of course, a couple of lads from school, a couple of girls I think he'd been good friends with from work and of course the team. His mum was inconsolable. She started crying before the coffin was even lowered into the ground. Swifty's dad held her and she cried onto his shoulder. I'd never seen the team so sombre either.

It was a weird atmosphere. Have you ever been to a funeral? Of course, your Grandad's six months before you met me. Then you know what it's like.

We drove in silence to The Function Room that the Swift's had hired out for the wake. I've been there once before, one of my mate's twenty-first years ago. Nice place, your kind of place. I think Mr Swift knew the owners, so they'd given him the room for free or something.

Yozzer was right. An Irish wake was something else. Everyone seemed to forget that it was a sad occasion and we drank like we had just won the cup final. It wasn't like people weren't thinking about Swifty either, it's just… I guess it was a celebration rather than a funeral, you know. Like we were celebrating his life and everything instead of being sad that we wouldn't get to do anything else with him ever again.

'OK, men, let's say goodbye to Swifty the best way we know,' Skip said to us after God knows how many pints of the Black Stuff.

'What do you mean?' I asked. Yozzer looked at me and then Skip, clearly equally confused.

'We're gonna sing him away.'

'Yes, let's do it,' Mac said, unbuttoning his shirt. Coach and a few of the others were also starting to remove their tops. Now, I don't know what you're going to think of this. Probably think it's some stupid rugby thing. Though maybe you'll love this. I don't know any more what you might like. Anyway, this was special.

'Just follow me,' Skip said. I looked at Yozzer and one of his eyebrows was still raised. Then he shrugged and took off his shirt. Skip had gone over to the DJ and was whispering something into his ear.

'Come on, mate. Let's just do it,' Yozzer said.

'Okay…' I said, slowly removing my tie and shirt. I'm glad I did

'Right men, time to wave off Swifty the Phoenix way. With respect to his family, who have come all the way over from Ireland, feel free to join us. You all remember what Swifty sang a couple of years ago at karaoke night?' Skip said through the

DJ's mic as the music faded out. I looked around. The Function room was packed. More people had arrived, those that couldn't make the actual funeral and friends that weren't as close to Swifty. Around thirty men in total had removed their shirts. Yozzer grabbed my arm and we went to the front. Skip nodded to the DJ and music started play. I couldn't quite make it out until a mass of voice's started singing.

'I MET MY LOVE, AT THE GAS WORKS WALL!' they sang, a collection of fists in the air. Yozzer and I joined in. 'DREAMED A DREAM, BY THE OLD CANAL! I KISSED MY GIRL, BY THE FACTORY WALL. DIRTY OLD TOWN, DIRTY OLD TOWN!'

People had their phones out and they were filming us. I could see Mrs Swift crying again, but this time she had a smile on her face. She was singing as well. Mr Swift had removed his shirt and joined us, along with his cousins. Halfway through we put our arms around each other. I couldn't hold it in anymore and started to cry. Yozzer had his arm around me and as the song died out a cheer went up. People were clapping and I kept crying. Skip and Mac and others came around me as all the men embraced and hugged each other.

'You were a good mate to him,' Skip said to me. 'Don't forget that. You're a good kid.'

The wake went on for hours. At one point, not sure when, Yozzer and I went out the front and sat on a nearby bench.. The good thing about today was I hadn't thought about Alicia, until I realised I hadn't thought about her. I checked my phone but of course she hadn't messaged me. Why would she? She wanted nothing to do with me. Like you now.

'I miss you,' I wrote on a message to her, then put the phone down without sending it. Yozzer pulled out two mini bottles of Jameson from his blazer. It's something we rarely drank but today felt appropriate.

'I've saved these all day. Drink it and give me your phone,' he said.

'Why?'

'Cause you'll message her. I know you better than you think.'

'Fine,' I said. I pressed send, then closed the window. I wish now I hadn't sent it.

'I'm not thick, Taz. I know you will have already messaged her. But we'll have a couple more here and you'll end up sending more drunken messages.'

'OK, OK,' I smiled. We clinked glasses. 'To Swifty.'

'Hell of a send-off,' Yozzer said. I nodded. We drank in silence. Neither of us needed to say anything. We were both thinking of the same thing. We did indeed have a couple more and then I came home, remembering only at the last second to get my phone from Yozzer. What a day today has been. Emotional to say the least. But I got through it Shona. Without you, without Alicia, just with my boys and by myself. Maybe I will be OK.

Jamie.

***

Pre-Game Fat Burners:	4
Minutes Played:	0
Times I left the Bench:	3
Number Worn:	20

Dear Shona,

This letter is going to be difficult to write. For one, I'm in hospital. Secondly, I've done something stupid. Very stupid. I woke up here yesterday and have spent most of the time trying to piece together what happened. Yozzer has filled me in on a lot of it as well. I don't want to worry you, but I have to tell you. I saw Alicia. Why don't I just start from Saturday morning and I'll do my best to tell it as best as I can remember. More and more keeps coming back to me. I never get bad memory loss, so hopefully I'll be able to tell you anything.

I'd been dropped. I couldn't complain really, after my last performance the other week. So for this game I was sat on the touch line in the interchange. It was doubtful I'd even get on at all. My entire body was not responding. It felt heavy and useless. My legs didn't want to move much beyond walking pace. Now some dickhead in a head guard who Skip had played with at Thatto had gone onto Swifty's wing and the young lad who had slotted in there was at full back.

He was OK, I suppose.

We won by about twenty points, but I didn't feel like celebrating with the lads. In the changing room I threw my shirt into the pile in the middle and went into the shower before anyone else. Yozzer appeared a few seconds later.

'You doing all right, pal?' he asked.

'Fine.'

'You sure?'

'Yozzer, I'm fine.'

'Gonna have a few bevvies?'

'Probably not.'

'Come on mate, I'll buy you one. Just don't go straight home.'

'I'm not thirsty.'

'It's not your thirst I'm worried about.'

He meant me. He gave a shit and I believed him. It was strangely morbid to be thankful for someone's concern, I don't want to be a burden on anyone, but just the fact that someone cared made me feel that one drink might not be so bad.

But of course, it wasn't just one drink.

I drank the first pint quickly. Five minutes later, I had downed the second. The third lasted less than a minute.

'Slow down mate, I aint spending the night in A and E with you getting ya stomach pumped!' Yozzer said, three quarters of the way down his first drink.

'I'm only having a couple,' I said, ordering my fourth Boddys.

'A couple is two mate…'

'Don't be so pedantic.'

'Seriously though, slow it down a little.'

'Jesus Christ, Yozzer, you're the one who told me to have a drink. So I'm having a drink!'

Yozzer looked as though he was about to tear me a new one when suddenly I felt Mac's big fat arm around my shoulder.

'Boys, Punch Tarmey after here, me missus's birthday.'

'No thank you,' I said, shaking his arm off me.

'We'll be there,' Yozzer said, pulling me away. He took me out to the balcony and towards the corner where no one else was. Inside the clubhouse, the Port Corner Bell rang.

'Look mate, I know you're struggling, so I'm not gonna have a go, but don't be a dick to us.'

'I'm not being a dick,' I protested. But I was, and I knew it. Since Swifty's funeral I'd gone back into my shell and now I was being a twat.

'You're taking it out on us. I get it, you find it harder than us. I miss Swifty too though. And yeah, losing Alicia aint been good either, but stop letting the fact that that cunt turned her back on you get in between you and me and the rest of the team.'

I was shocked. Yozzer had never spoken to me like that before. Yet, I still got defensive, 'Don't call her a cunt, mate.'

'She is though! Yes, I understand you got intense, and that you acted like a tool when you were drunk a couple of times. But she knew exactly how you were. She knew that you had issues and she knew that you were struggling, and she knew about Swifty! So I'm sorry mate, but she's a cunt.'

I had no comeback. None at all. Your good mates will take the piss, and will get smashed with you, and have a laugh with you, but your best mates will put you in your place. I loved the bastard. It had never crossed my mind that's what I probably needed. Just a reminder of how Alicia had treated me, rather than thinking about how *I* treated *her*. I hugged him and he hugged me back.

'Get a room you benders,' someone shouted over. We laughed and turned around to see it was Samoa. He was smiling, 'get over here and let's have a game of nails before we go to Mac's missus's do.'

'Is your missus going?' Yozzer asked.

'She's never coming anywhere near you perverts ever again.'

I laughed. Samoa's girlfriend was fit as and we all knew it. Even you would have a crush on her, Shona. She had come down to watch a game once. She got Man of the Match and serenaded in the club afterwards by the entire team. We sang her *Lady in Red*. It was kind of a tradition when a new girl was brought up here. Remember when we did it you? You loved it and I don't blame you. Probably good Alicia never got that treatment. Before I could start to fall back into the spiral, the hammer was being thrust into my hands and a nail positioned in the log.

Somehow, I came second.

The taxis came to get us an hour or so later. I'd slowed my drinking down, much to the delight of Yozzer. I say he was being a good friend, well he was, but he also didn't like being out drunk by me, though I was already steaming. Just something he'd have to deal with to be honest. At Punch Tarmey we got on the Guinness. I bought Mac's missus a drink, a white wine spritzer, to say happy birthday. Seeing as she did most of the teas during the season it was the least I could do for her. You remember her, right? Nice lady. I was feeling better, Yozzer was doing a good job of that. So were the rest of the team to be honest. The air of Swifty was still around, which was comforting, and nice that people weren't forgetting him instantly. Players were still dropping his name into conversation like 'remember that try Swifty scored' or 'Swifty was always breaking ankles with his steps'. I liked this. I finished my first pint here and Yozzer offered to get the next one, so I took the

173

opportunity to take a slash.

Then I saw her.

I don't know how long she had been here. Probably since before we arrived. I would have noticed her if she had arrived after us, she'd have had to walk past us. She was sat on the table with some musclebound, roided up bellend. You know the sort. I remember him well. Pretty boy with point-five percent body fat, perfect hair and perfect tan, tattoos that had no meaning down his arms and a smile that you wanted to punch clean off. She had her usual gin and tonic and he had a Carling. Poof. They were both laughing at something one of them had said and her hand was on his arm.

Her eyes caught mine. Her laugh dropped down to a smile. The arsehole she was sat with noticed and looked over. Then he looked down at the table and away. The bastard knew exactly who I was. But I didn't know him. She took a deep breath and whispered something to the prick. They drank what was left of their drinks, got up and left. I watched them walk out together.

In my stomach, a razorblade was whirling. It was spinning around, jumping and gyrating, slashing away at my intestines. My hands became fists. My breathing quickened and I could feel my nostrils flare.

Are you kidding me? The selfish bitch. The liar. The cunt.

Now is where things get hazy, but I'll do my best. I've just remembered more. I was storming down the street and away from Punch Tarmey's. Part of me wanted to find them. My own personal self-harm. Part of me wanted to get away. The rest of me was fighting with which emotion I should be feeling. There was anger, there was jealousy and there was pain. Not to mention I was drunk. So I just walked as tears started to flow.

I couldn't take it anymore. Damn, the pain in my stomach was excruciating. Even when she called it a day, it didn't hurt this much. Was it the lie that she wasn't seeing anyone? Was it the pure jealousy?

Or was it that she didn't want anything to do with me when I needed her the most?

I don't know how long I'd been walking for, but it must have been close to an hour, because I could see the train tracks ahead of me. A sudden piece of inspiration hit me. That would end the hurt. I'm not proud of this, Shona, but I climbed the fence and stood in the middle of the tracks. I didn't know which way to face. The train could come from either direction. I picked a direction and raised my arms.

'Come on then!' I shouted, 'come on you piece of shit. Do it! Come on, where are ya?'

I remember falling to my knees, tears once again streaming down my face.

'Please. Please, end it for me. Just fucking end it.'

I was there for what seemed like forever, but it could only have been five or so minutes. No train was coming. I looked at my phone, a message from Yozzer.

'Where did you go?'

There were three missed calls from him and just as I was about to put my phone away it buzzed again.

'Pal, I'm worried, where are you?'

I put my phone in my pocket before I thought about drunkenly messaging Alicia. I should have replied to Yozzer and get him to come and get me. Then I got off the train tracks and stumbled over the fence. I had no idea where I was. I just walked in the direction I came, hoping I would recognise somewhere soon. It must have been another hour of aimless walking, my head scrambled as I thought about Alicia riding that muscled guy. In my head, she was grinding on him hard, squealing and screaming in pleasure as he gave her multiple orgasms. Then he flipped her over and fucked her from behind, sweat on his tattoos, slapping her arse she screamed louder and louder and she came over and over and over again.

Why do we do that to ourselves? I did it with you once. I heard a month after we split you'd started dating someone else and all I could think about for a week was you and him. I'd think about you on dates with some perfect man, fucking him nightly. Ah, even the thought now gets to me.

I somehow ended up outside my flat. The key somehow slipped into the lock and I stumbled up the stairs and into my flat. I fell into my bedroom and onto my bed. Pulling my phone out of my pocket I felt it vibrate as yet another missed call from Yozzer. I tossed the phone on the bed and looked at my bedside table.

And there they were.

My anti-depressants. Citalopram, 40mg film coated tablets. Four whole packets worth, with the days of the week over each one, in two rows. That's four weeks' worth, 80mg a day. There was a bottle of water next to it. But no, I needed something else.

Here it is Shona. You don't have to read this. Even writing it I'm finding it tough. In fact I feel shame and depression rising up. I'm sorry if you find it difficult to read. I know how stupid I was. Most of this is a blur, but this is the jist.

In the kitchen there was an unopened bottle of Sailor Jerry's Spiced Rum. Back in my bedroom I pulled out the cork and popped a pill. It slid down my throat nice and easy. But nothing happened. Why wasn't it working? That's not how they work, of course. But I was drunk. And in so much pain. I wanted the pain to stop as I started to blubber once more.

So I popped another pill.

It didn't work.

I popped another.

Still nothing.

I popped another.

And another.

And another.

I tossed the empty packet across my room. Fourteen pills and nothing.

So I did the second packet. Twenty-eight pills and nothing.

Forty-two.

Fifty-six.

I opened the drawer and pulled out another packet and started popping them. The world started to go blurry. I may well have grabbed another packet, I can't remember. From what the doctors told me I probably did. In the distance, somewhere, I heard someone's voice.

'Mate, you left your door open, I've been trying to call you,' it sounded a bit like Yozzer, but I couldn't be sure, the world was starting to go dark, 'TAZ! TAZ WHAT THE HELL ARE YOU DOING…?!'

The darkness started to close around me. The world was going a million miles an hour. My stomach, suddenly was no longer in pain from Alicia, but in physical pain. My head was spinning like the Whirlitzer at the funfair. I thought the pain earlier was excruciating, it had nothing on this. Someone was beside me, shouting something. I don't know what, they were shaking me, I think. All I can remember from this point is the pain. I was hoping I'd just pass out.

Thinking back now, did I really intend to kill myself? The answer is yes, I did. I wanted to die. I wanted it all to go away. I wanted the pain to stop. I mean I hurt now, but I can deal with that. Was it selfish? Maybe. But it's my life. I couldn't do it anymore and on Saturday I just wanted to end it all. No more pain. No more thoughts of Alicia. No more missing Swifty. No more letters to you.

Jamie.

***

St Helens Hospital, August 14th

Dear Shona,

Do you remember that trip we took to Lytham St Annes to visit your cousin? You went up by yourself and I came up to surprise you a couple of days later. It was over the Challenge Cup Final weekend. I remember because we watched it in a pub together and sat next to a guy who coached his son's rugby team. Think it was called The Taps. Do you remember?

It's funny the things you think about when you're unconscious. I thought I'd be thinking of Alicia, playing out the scenario in my head repeatedly. But I haven't been, I've been thinking about you and our trip. Your cousin had that nice house looking out onto the green by the seafront. Well, I'm willing to bet they still have that house. Why would you sell up and move?

What was the name of that Mediterranean restaurant we had tapas in? I can't remember at all what it was called. It was so nice. The weather was amazing as well. It was August then as well, must have been if the cup final was on. We walked along the seafront, the wind blowing nicely, keeping us cool but not so that we were all over the place.

Do you remember?

I thought I'd forgotten if I'm honest. But whilst I was out, or in a coma, whatever the hell it was, I was thinking about it. My favourite memory is when I saw you lean on the barrier looking out over the beach and sea and your hair was whipping around you and your eyes were squinting in the sun. You were smiling. It was then that I knew I was in love with you.

And it made me realise what a mistake I actually made. I think part of me had masked that out. Put some kind of covering over it. Thrust it right to the back of my head. It was still there, waiting for something to pull it forward. Looks like it was my effort at ending my life that did that.

All those suicidal thoughts I'd had all just built up. Losing Swifty and Alicia, along with the feeling that I wasn't over losing you, all just come to a front. I was always concerned I'd lost you to someone else, always so paranoid, I guess that when I saw Alicia with someone else it triggered all that paranoia into actions. Deep down somewhere, I was thinking people will just up and leave me. Swifty did it, you did it and now Alicia had done it. And that fear turned into actions.

When I think about the attempt, I sometimes try to reason with myself that it wasn't suicide. I try to tell myself that I was just trying to numb that pain. But that's just an excuse. Of course, I knew what would happen if I swallowed that amount of drugs. It was an OD and it was an attempt on my life. I didn't want to be here anymore. And if Yozzer hadn't been the best friend he was then I wouldn't be.

It hurt, it really hurt. I mean I won't be doing it again in a hurry. Some people say they self-harm because they can deal with physical pain more than emotional. I would much rather cry into a pillow over lost love or my friend or my loneliness than do that again. My stomach is still in pieces.

This, Shona, is going to be the last letter I write you. Whether I actually send these out or not, who knows. Maybe one day we'll talk about it and you can read what happened. Or maybe I'll just burn the lot. Or, and this is more likely, I'll bury them somewhere where I'll never find them. I'm going to go to therapy and I've already started talking to people. That's one suggestion they gave me.

Before I end this though, I want to tell you about Yozzer. He, along with Swifty, is the best friend I've ever had. He can come across like an asshole, but he was there. Call it lucky timing if you want, I call it being a damn good friend. He saw the spiral and he was there. I should have listened to him more and I will do from now on. My best friend. When I needed him, he was there. Same with the rest of the Phoenix team to be honest. They were all there. Swifty's funeral will go down forever as a family coming together. I'll have that image of us all chanting and dancing, our shirts off, for the rest of my life. Apparently, the video is going viral.

When I actually get out of my own head I'll see how nice it is out there. Those boys, Yozzer, Mac, Skip, Samoa, Coach, even Newbie, all of them, they will always be there. Even if one of them buggers off somewhere or retires and becomes one of the 'Old Boys' they'll be there. They've all come to visit whilst I've been in hospital. Alicia hasn't. Apparently she heard, Yozzer got hold of her and told her. But the boys, they all came. Mac brought flowers. It was a joke, he was trying to call me a girl. It worked, I laughed and so did Yozzer. The nurse thought it was poor taste. I thought it was brilliant. I didn't want sympathy. I didn't need sympathy. I needed my friends and I needed them to be just that. And they were. I needed that banter back.

I'll be out of hospital soon, but now I have been told I *have* to go to therapy. They've given me a counsellor and I have to come back to the hospital every week to see them. I don't mind, I think it is for the best anyway. I just can't wait to get back on the rugby field. It won't be this season, I highly doubt it, but it'll be soon, I hope. Even if I have to start in the interchange.

I'll come off the steroids as well as they didn't really help. Plus, after having my stomach pumped and barely eating for goodness knows how long I've lost a bit of mass anyway. I had to be honest with the doctors because they took blood tests. Something else that I can talk to the counsellor about. As for Yozzer, he wasn't happy about the 'roids, but he understood.

Anyway, I think it's time I said goodbye. Maybe one day we will meet again and be able to talk and it not be a problem. Maybe one day we'll bump into each other in Asda and you'll ask me; 'how are things?' and I'll be able to say; 'you know what Shona? I'm great.' One day, hopefully.

All my love,

Jamie.

THE END